No, he wasn't a stranger. His face was familiar, of course it was, and she'd think of his name in a minute. In a minute she'd remember....

But his name never came to her. And suddenly she was afraid.

"Who are you?" she whispered.

He stopped dead. If his face had been unrevealing before, it was flatly blank now.

"Seth," he said slowly. "Seth Brogan."

She closed her mouth. Licked her dry lips. Stared at him as if she could force her way through his deliberate blankness, force her way through to what she desperately needed. And asked her next question.

"Who am I?"

Dear Reader,

It's hard to believe that this is the grand finale of CELEBRATION 1000! But all good things must come to an end. Not that there aren't more wonderful things in store for you next month, too....

But as for June, first we have an absolutely sizzling MAN OF THE MONTH from Ann Major called *The Accidental Bodyguard*.

Are you a fan of HAWK'S WAY? If so, don't miss the latest "Hawk's" story, *The Temporary Groom* by Joan Johnston. Check out the family tree on page six and see if you recognize all the members of the Whitelaw family.

And with *The Cowboy and the Cradle* Cait London has begun a fabulous new western series—THE TALLCHIEFS. (P.S. The next Tallchief is all set for September!)

Many of you have written to say how much you love Elizabeth Bevarly's books. Her latest, *Father of the Brood*, book #2 in the FROM HERE TO PATERNITY series, simply shouldn't be missed.

This month is completed with Karen Leabo's *The Prodigal Groom,* the latest in our WEDDING NIGHT series, and don't miss a wonderful star of tomorrow— DEBUT AUTHOR Eileen Wilks, who's written *The Loner and the Lady*.

As for next month...we have a not-to-be-missed MAN OF THE MONTH by Anne McAllister, and Dixie Browning launches DADDY KNOWS LAST, a new Silhouette continuity series beginning in Desire.

Lucia Macro

Senior Editor

Please address questions and book requests to:
Silhouette Reader Service
U.S.: 3010 Walden Ave., P.O. Box 1325, Buffalo, NY 14269
Canadian: P.O. Box 609, Fort Erie, Ont. L2A 5X3

EILEEN WILKS
THE LONER AND THE LADY

SILHOUETTE *Desire®*
Published by Silhouette Books
America's Publisher of Contemporary Romance

This one has to be for Karen.

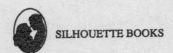 SILHOUETTE BOOKS

ISBN 0-373-76008-6

THE LONER AND THE LADY

Copyright © 1996 by Eileen Wilks

Printed in U.S.A.

EILEEN WILKS

is a fifth-generation Texan. Her great-great-grandmother came to Texas in a covered wagon shortly after the end of the Civil War—excuse us, the War Between the States. But she's not a full-blooded Texan. Right after another war, her Texan father fell for a Yankee woman. This obviously mismatched pair proceeded to travel to nine cities in three countries in the first twenty years of their marriage, raising two kids and innumerable dogs and cats along the way. For the next twenty years they stayed put, back home in Texas again—and still together.

Eileen figures her professional career matches her nomadic upbringing, since she tried everything from drafting to a brief stint as a ranch hand—raising two children and any number of cats and dogs along the way. Not until she started writing did she "stay put," because that's when she knew she'd come home.

Dear Reader,

I love to write Desires for the same reasons I love to read them. They're fast, spicy, varied, and give me characters I want to spend time with. Many of my favorite authors are found within Desire's red covers. So when my editor told me my book would be part of the big birthday party Desire is throwing to celebrate its 1000th book, I went up like a rocket. The only reason I can't call it a dream come true is because it hadn't occurred to me to dream so big. Being part of a celebration headlined by authors whose books I've cherished for years is like being a rookie invited to step up to the plate in the fourth inning of the World Series—scary, thrilling, absolutely wonderful.

I didn't plan to write *The Loner and the Lady*. For a couple weeks I'd been trying to begin a different book, but I was trapped in the first chapter. Finally I cleared my computer screen. "This isn't working," I said. "What do I really want to write?" I found myself with Seth on a mountain in the middle of a storm, looking for a lost dog—and amazed when he discovered another sort of stray.

The Loner and the Lady turned out to be what I really wanted to write. I've always had a weakness for dark, brooding heroes, so I loved the time I spent with Seth and Sophie. I hope you will, too.

Eileen Wilks

One

Only a fool would be out on a night like this, Seth Brogan thought, scowling as the wind lashed rain in under the brim of his Stetson and sent another rivulet running under the neck of his slicker. Only a fool would come out on the mountain in this weather, looking for a stupid female that didn't have enough sense to stay home when a storm threatened.

Seth's drenched jeans chafed his skin with every step he took along the uneven path. His left thigh ached the way it always did in the cold these days, but so far, at least, it wasn't seizing up on him. Now if he could just find that bitch—his foot slipped in the mud and he cursed—find her before she started dropping those pups. She had to be nearly due, the way her stomach practically dragged the ground.

"Rocky!" he hollered, but the wind snatched the dog's name out of his mouth so quickly he hardly heard it himself.

Nothing. His frown tightened down another notch. As he followed the murky beam from his flashlight farther up the path a rock shifted underfoot, nearly sending him down.

So he was a fool. What else was new?

He rounded the big boulder that he'd named Mama Bear soon after finding this refuge. His light stabbed beneath the overhang he'd been aiming for, where an ugly yellow dog lay on the sheltered dirt, panting cheerfully.

When lightning seared the sky, he had about one second's warning. One second to hear something crashing through the scrub to his right, something large and very close, its approach hidden in the maelstrom of wind and renewed darkness after the lightning's glare. Barely enough time to turn and brace himself.

"What the hell!"

Thunder boomed about two feet above his head. He reached out and caught the slim form that ran and fell right into him—caught it by its shoulders as another fork of lightning stabbed the sky. In the stark, actinic brilliance he saw that he held a woman, a young woman, with fear-blank eyes and blood—oh, Lord. Blood, black as sin in the brief dazzle of light, covered the side of her face.

Thunder followed lightning as fast as the tail follows the dog. The woman jerked under the onslaught of noise and threw herself up against him.

Seth froze in astonishment so complete that, for one foolish moment, the storm ceased to exist. She'd come right *at* him, right up into his arms as if she hadn't seen him. Well, he realized, as his arm moved belatedly to steady the frightened creature plastered against his chest, obviously she hadn't seen his face as clearly as he'd seen hers. Too scared, and maybe halfway into shock.

He felt the sigh that shuddered through her as his arm tightened around her. With that exhalation, she went limp.

He damned near dropped her. She wasn't all that heavy, but the startling nearness of her, the foreign sensation of touch, dulled his reactions. Clutching her body tighter to him, he searched out the tender spot under her jaw with his other hand. The skin there was sticky with her blood, but he felt the rhythm of her heartbeat, a little too fast but strong enough.

Thank God.

He'd never get her into a proper carry, not when he had to keep hold of the flashlight to have any hope of making it back down to the cabin. But once in a while his size came in handy. He bent, tucked his shoulder into her stomach and stood. His knee protested sharply. He looked over his un-burdened shoulder. "Dammit, dog," he yelled over the wind, "come on!"

Rocky didn't always come when he called her. She was a stray, after all, and didn't know him that well, though she'd hung around for a month now. Seth started down the path. He didn't look back. But his heart gave a relieved thump when he felt a fat, warm body press up against his legs.

"Good dog," he said, though she probably couldn't hear him over the storm. "Good girl."

By the time he reached the cabin, his knee ached steadily and his calf muscles burned and twitched. He knew what that meant. *Not much longer,* he mentally told his leg as he staggered with his limp burden onto the covered porch that ran along the front of the cabin. *Hold up a few more minutes,* he told the throbbing muscles as he limped into the cabin's one large room.

He'd been too low on fuel the past couple days to run the generator, so the only light was a fitful reddish glow from the fireplace in the center of the big, undivided room. It was enough for him to steer his way to the sleeping area on the opposite side of the room, but once there he didn't dare bend to set her down on the oversize bed. His knee might buckle and he'd fall over on top of her. So he more or less dropped her onto the quilt-covered mattress.

His calf spasmed. "Ah, hell," he gasped, sinking to one knee, his bad leg stretched out straight. The muscles of his face clenched almost as tightly as the ones knotting his calf as he rubbed the leg. After a moment the spasm eased.

He needed to get the leg warm and stay off it. He knew that but couldn't do it yet. With a grimace he pulled himself onto the bed beside her and laid his fingers on her throat to check the pulse—still rapid, but was it a little weaker?

He had to get her warm before she went into shock. He threw the bed covers over her, then stood and limped back to the door to shut out the rain.

Rocky had curled up in her favorite spot, the rag rug in front of the fireplace. "Sorry, old girl," he said to the dog watching him curiously. "I know you don't like closed doors any more than I do, but we've got to get this place heated up for whoever is bleeding all over my bed."

Seth hung the slicker onto its peg and tossed his Stetson on the table by the door. When he did, the strip of cloth he'd used to tie his hair back came out. He muttered under his breath but didn't bother retying it as he grabbed his first aid kit and two kerosene lanterns.

He lit the lanterns and set one on the table by the bed, the other on the shelf above it. Extra blankets came from the chest at the foot of the bed. His kit went on the floor beside him. Then there was nothing left to do but tend her, and for the first time since moving to the mountain, Seth regretted his refusal to have a phone line run to the cabin. Not that help could have reached them. The storm would render the road impassable for days, and no helicopter could fly in this weather. But he could have talked to a physician, gotten some backup. It had been a long time since he'd used any part of his training.

Her lapse into unconsciousness worried him. A subdural hematoma could send a person into coma hours after the original blow to the head, even if they'd been up and lucid afterward. He checked her pulse again. It was still fast, which didn't indicate hematoma but might presage shock. She was very pale. Even the warm glow of the lanterns hadn't put any color in her face.

It was a lovely face. Delicate. He couldn't help noticing that as he pulled the penlight from his kit. She had a dainty little nose, and lips that were probably pretty when they weren't all cracked and colorless. He peeled back one of her eyelids, shining his light directly into her eye. The pupil contracted quickly. He let the lid close again.

Even her coloring was delicate. Her eyebrows arched in perfect, pastel half-moons above her closed eyes. Pale lashes rested, motionless, against her bleached cheeks, and short blond hair clung to her scalp like mud.

He checked the other eye. Her pupils responded evenly, thank God.

Blood covered one side of that pretty face. He hesitated briefly—his kit was fairly complete but lacked disposable gloves, since he'd never expected to treat anyone but himself with it. Still, what choice was there? Leaving her untended wasn't an option.

He explored the left side of her head carefully and found a swelling above her temple, then began cleaning away the blood so he could see where she was hurt. She stirred but didn't wake. He found several lacerations. It looked as if she'd fallen and scraped or torn the skin on a rough surface. None of the scrapes were deep enough to worry about, and the cuts had pretty much stopped bleeding.

Time for a proper reading of her pulse and pressure. He cuffed her and timed the pulse, watching her chest rise and fall as he counted. Respiration shallow but not too fast, which was good. Pulse over ninety... bad. Blood pressure at the low end of normal. Skin chilly to the touch.

She wasn't in shock yet. But she was in danger of it. He had to get her warm and pray there was no internal bleeding.

She sure wasn't dressed for the mountains. Or for a storm. Her sleeveless green top and full pants looked dressy. They had the sheen of silk, too. Linda had worn a lot of silk, expensive things like this. Whatever this woman's outfit had cost originally, though, it was useless now, muddy and torn.

The top buttoned down the front with those aggravating little cloth-covered buttons that women like. Her skin beneath the cloth had a disturbing chill, and his big fingers made slow work of those blasted buttons. So he quit trying to preserve her ruined clothes and tore the top open.

She had beautiful breasts.

Seth didn't stop, couldn't stop in the middle of stripping her chilled body to stare, but he couldn't keep from looking, either. To save him he couldn't have stopped looking.

She was soft and white and...perfect. From the coral tips of her breasts, nicely peaked from the cold, to the way her slender waist flared into the curve of her hips, to the pretty nest of curls at the top of her thighs, she was the most perfectly shaped woman he'd ever seen.

Or maybe I've just forgotten, he thought, lips tight with anger at himself when he realized he'd been so busy gawking at her that he'd forgotten to take her shoes off before pulling down her slacks and panties. Her well-worn running shoes sure didn't go with the rest of her outfit. Quickly he pulled the knotted laces free, jerked the shoes off and finished stripping her.

It had been so long. So very long.

He removed everything—socks, watch and a dainty little locket on a chain, dropping them in the pile with her clothes. But he kept his touch impersonal as he checked her as quickly as he could for any injuries that had been hidden by her clothing.

No detectable damage. He could hope that meant he'd found everything. He wrapped her carefully in a blanket, struck with a ridiculous sense of loss when her lovely body was covered. Changing the damp bedding beneath her didn't take long. By the time he had her settled between clean sheets and fresh blankets with her legs slightly elevated by pillows, her skin was warming, though her color was still bad.

He waited a few minutes, rubbing his knee, then took another blood pressure reading. The results told him plainly that she was responding to the increased warmth, which meant it was unlikely she had any internal hemorrhaging. Relief swamped him.

He decided to get an antibiotic dressing on the facial lacerations. When he applied it, though, she jerked away, dislodging the covers. He paused, waiting to see if she'd wake. Almost hoping she wouldn't. Because then she'd see him.

"I'm sorry," he whispered, and he meant for everything he was and wasn't, everything he'd thought but hadn't done when he looked at her. His hand lingered for a moment, just a moment, on her soft flesh before he tugged the covers up and stood.

First he added a couple of logs to the fire. Then he got out of his own wet things, rubbed himself dry briskly and pulled on jeans and a shirt he didn't bother to button. He filled the coffeepot with water and hung it from the hook over the fire.

It was going to be a long night. He'd have to keep an eye on her, try to wake her every hour or so.

He looked over her clothing as he spread it out on the hearth to dry, noting the designer label hand-stitched inside. Damp sheets and quilts went anywhere he found a spot for them. Good thing he didn't intend to sleep anytime soon. There wasn't a dry blanket in the place, except for those covering her.

He pulled the big, handmade rocker next to the hearth in the sleeping area and sat, heaving a sigh of relief. His knee and calf ached badly, but he hoped the heat from the fire would help enough that he wouldn't be too crippled up tomorrow.

He held up her watch and necklace, examining the mellow gold in the glow of firelight. Both were expensive. Neither told him why a woman like her was out in the wilderness at midnight, bloody and wounded.

An automobile accident? It wasn't completely consistent with her injuries—the lump on her head was in the wrong place, for one thing—but it was all he could think of just then. Highway 142 did lie on the other side of Old Baldy, and the climb wasn't a difficult one—in dry, daylit weather, for a hiker in good shape. Hard to believe she'd crossed Old

Baldy's slopes in the middle of a thunderstorm, at night, with an injury to her head.

He glanced at the bed where she lay, a small, helpless lump under the blankets. He had no business, no business whatsoever, remembering what she looked like without the covers, without any covering at all. He'd better remember that. Because she was going to wake up. That was the only acceptable alternative. She was going to look at him and realize he'd undressed her, that he'd seen her.

She'd probably hate him for that.

His hand lifted absently to stroke the scar tissue on the left side of his face, scarring that ran down his neck to his shoulder and splashed across the top of his chest. Life wasn't like fairy tales. The woman in his bed wasn't going to like knowing that the Beast had looked on her beauty.

Pain came in colors and textures. At the bottom of the ocean, pain was mostly pressure, a distant, enveloping purple, but as she drew nearer the surface, pain turned a crackly, yellowish green.

A bruise-colored feeling. That was the surface, and she didn't want to go there, not yet. Not when the pain was still so strong. But something, someone, was calling her, pulling her reluctantly nearer... gradually she realized the pain came from her head. It hurt. Completely. Relentlessly. And there was something else... all at once she remembered terror, and fought her way up and out.

Her eyes opened. Someone groaned. And above her, bending over her...

He was big. His inky dark hair hung loose around his face, and his eyes were as black as his hair. His skin was rough, as were the features in his narrow face, and half of his face was ruined.

And she knew him. He'd come to her out of the terrible darkness, catching her when she fell, stopping her flight with his big arms. She remembered seeing his face in the white flare of lightning, seeing his eyes, black and liquid as the night around them, seeing the ruined side of his face and thinking that he was hurt, too, hurt like her. With a sigh of relief she closed her eyes and let herself sink back down, knowing she was safe. Because he was here.

Seth stared down at the woman in his bed. She'd woken. She was going to be all right. She'd woken and seen him . . . And smiled.

She woke to the smell of food cooking and the sound of bird song. Dreams and nightmares sluiced off her like water as she surfaced, a swimmer rising from murky depths. Her head hurt worse than it ever had in her life, and her bladder was miserably full. When she cracked open her eyes, light seeped in like pain.

Bacon? Did she smell bacon frying?

She looked around without turning her head. Moving would definitely be a mistake. The light wasn't really very bright, she realized as her eyes focused. The closest window showed a dim, rainy day outside, though that didn't seem to discourage the noisy chorus of birds. Inside was a cabin, a real log cabin with the walls planed smooth and varnished in some places, left rough in others. The effect was unusual but pleasing. She looked up at a high ceiling of glossy boards. The big bed she was in pointed her feet at a fireplace in the center of the room, circled by a low, brick hearth.

Something—no, someone—was missing. Someone who had been taking care of her. "I, uh . . ." She stopped and tried to swallow. Her throat was as dry as her bladder was full.

He moved into her range of vision from somewhere near her feet. He was big—one of those really big men who, she thought with a slow blink, when seen from a distance, don't look unusually large because everything is in balance. He didn't make a sound as he came to stand next to her bed and looked down at her.

Her eyes drifted up to his face. His dark hair hung loose below his jaw line. Livid scar tissue covered him from the crest of his cheekbone on down past his jaw, his neck, disappearing under the collar of his plain blue work shirt. The skin was shiny smooth, the angry color left by bad burns. The scarring distracted her.

Then she noticed the way his hands were knotted into fists at his sides. "What's wrong?" she croaked, alarmed. Was she even sicker, more damaged, than her pounding head suggested?

His big hands relaxed. "I didn't know if you were completely awake this time." His voice matched the rest of him, deep and solid and vaguely reassuring.

"How long...?"

"You've been out for over fifteen hours," he said, sitting on the bed beside her. "I think you've just been sleeping, though, not unconscious, since the last time I woke you. Where do you hurt?" He put his big hands on her neck and probed gently.

"My head." Fifteen hours. She tried, and failed, to think of what had happened to her.

"Anywhere else?" He prodded her lightly. "Here? Or here?"

"No." Why was she here, in this cabin, with him? The effort to think made the pounding in her head increase until it throbbed all the way along her jaw and down her neck. She gave up and closed her eyes. "I'm very thirsty."

The bed creaked as he shifted. "It should be okay for you to sit up for a drink. I'll have to lift you a bit," he said, and slid an arm carefully under her shoulders, supporting her neck. For all his care, it still hurt fiercely when he raised her off the pillow, and she made a small sound.

"Take it easy," he murmured, and held a glass to her lips. His low voice cooled the jagged edges of her pain the way the water soothed her dry throat. She managed several sips.

"Better?" he asked in that comforting voice as he laid her back down.

She thought about nodding and didn't. She thought about lying there until her other problem went away—but it wasn't going to. She forced her eyes open, wretchedly embarrassed. "I need to use the bathroom."

He nodded, the undamaged half of his face as unrevealing as the burned side. "I'll get a bowl for you to use as a bedpan."

"No way." Surely, if he helped her, she could make it to the bathroom. She couldn't stand the idea of some stranger, no matter how kind, helping her with such a private matter.

Some stranger?

No, he wasn't a stranger. He was . . . his face was familiar, of course it was, and she'd think of his name in a minute. In a minute she'd remember. . . .

By the time he came back to the bed, the humiliating bowl in his hand, her breath came in quick, fearful pants, like a dog. "Who are you?" she whispered.

He stopped dead. If his face had been unrevealing before, it was flatly blank now. "Seth," he said slowly. "Seth Brogan."

She closed her mouth. Licked her dry lips. Stared at him as if she could force her way through his deliberate blankness, force her way through to what she desperately needed. And asked her next question. "Who am I?"

Two

She couldn't remember?

Seth stood rooted to the floor, holding the stupid bowl. All he could think, selfishly, was that the fear he'd seen twisting her pallid face hadn't been about him, after all. She was afraid because she didn't remember who she was.

Finally he got his tongue unstuck. "A blow to the head can affect the memory, but it's temporary. Mostly temporary. You may never remember everything that happened right around your accident." If whatever happened to her had been an accident. He'd begun to have some doubts about that.

"But the rest—my name—will come back to me?"

"Sure," he said as if he knew the answer.

She wanted to believe him, that was obvious from the way her face relaxed. Then she saw the bowl in his hands and stiffened up again. "Are you a doctor?"

He shook his head.

She bit her lip. "I don't suppose you're my brother or something?"

He could have told her he was. She'd have accepted it. For some ungodly reason, probably because she had so little choice, she trusted him. Being cared for like this would be easier on her if she thought they were related.

Only how could he lie to her, when she trusted him? "Afraid not," he said. "But listen, it could be worse." The corner of his mouth, the one on the undamaged side, creaked up. "You could need a catheter. Trust me, that's worse."

In spite of everything, there was a faint, answering spark of humor in her eyes. Big, shamrock green eyes, he noticed for the first time. Green as the grass of Ireland, and somehow twice as pretty with the way her pale lashes left her eyes all open and unshielded.

Her humor died in the painful, awkward moments that followed. She hid by closing her eyes again. He went outside, leaving the door open so she could call him.

When he came back in she was white with pain and exhaustion, too worn-out, he thought, to feel more than mild embarrassment at their forced intimacy. He understood how that felt, too.

He had hoped she'd be able to get some soup down, but she fell asleep almost before he could get the covers settled back around her. Seth let his hands linger briefly while tucking her in, not invasively, he told himself. An innocent sort of touching, through the sheet and two blankets, and far less personal than the task he'd just performed for her.

But he looked at her face while his hands smoothed the covers over her. Her hair had dried to a streaky blond. It wisped around the edges of the pretty face eased by sleep, except on the left side. Dried blood clumped the soft blond strands together above her ear.

Looking at her sleeping face was, Seth understood, an invasion of sorts, an intrusion on her helplessness.

But he felt helpless, too. Helpless to keep from watching her. And wanting her, damn him for a fool. Seth looked over at the round oak table where he'd made a small pile of her things: slacks, panties, top, watch, a locket with a name engraved on it . . . and a small plastic bag he'd found in one of the deep pockets of that top. A bag half-full of white powder.

She woke up more easily this time, trailing wisps of memory after her. Enough memory to know where she was, so that she wasn't startled when she opened her eyes and saw rafters and wood above her. Dust motes danced in the sunbeam slanting in the window.

She didn't know what her name was. But she remembered his. "Seth?"

As before, he appeared almost immediately, his narrow face serious on one side, stiff with scars on the other. "How are you feeling?"

He wore jeans, a plain blue work shirt, and a dish towel stuck into the waist of his pants and apparently forgotten. The incongruously domestic touch on such a rough-looking man made her smile. "Better."

A lot better, she realized as she shifted, testing her body's reactions. Her head hurt, yes, but in a normal sort of way, no longer overpowering. Her whole body was stiff. She ached as if she'd been lying in one position far too long.

She breathed deeply and smelled a welcome aroma. "May I have a cup of that coffee?"

He hesitated. "I guess it wouldn't hurt. I'm out of milk, so I hope you take it black. Sugar?"

"I don't know." How very peculiar, not to know how she drank her coffee. And yet she'd known, when she smelled the coffee, that she wanted a cup. "You can give it to me without and we'll see if I like it that way."

"You don't seem very upset about your lack of memory."

She wasn't, and that, surely, was odd. But it was good just to lie here and not hurt. Too pleasant for her to waste energy worrying. She smiled. "I feel so much better than the last time I woke up, I guess it doesn't seem worth getting upset over. After all, like you said, my memories will come back soon."

He frowned. ''You'll need some breakfast to go with the coffee. I hope you like your eggs scrambled.''

''That sounds fine.'' Did she like scrambled eggs? Did she like eggs at all? The idea of eating them didn't disgust her, so she supposed they'd be okay.

When Seth moved she automatically followed him with her eyes, turning her head slightly on the pillow to keep him in sight.

Ouch. Well, it could be worse—had been, in fact, much worse. The swift stabbing pain that accompanied her head movement faded to the same dull ache she'd woken with. She ignored it in favor of studying the cabin...and Seth.

Seth was easy to watch. He got a bowl from the cabinets, moved out of her line of vision, and came back with several eggs cradled in one hand. He had big hands. Long fingers, like a pianist. He cracked the eggs into the bowl, stirred them, and carried the bowl to a large, modern stove, limping slightly.

She was curious about her rescuer, about his big hands and his big, athletically graceful body. Watching Seth was better than struggling with the clouds in her brain. Something about the way he moved, an athletic economy unimpaired by his limp, fascinated her, reminded her of—

Pain lanced through her skull, turning her so quickly away from the memory that she lost the thread of thought. She blinked, dazed, grateful for the easing of the pain.

She looked away from Seth and her fascination with him. When she moved her head again, cautiously, it didn't hurt too much, but her hair tugged at her scalp. She reached up and gingerly felt around the sorest place on her head, just above her left ear, and grimaced. Half her hair seemed to be caked together with what she was afraid was dried blood. Her blood.

She went back to her inspection of the cabin. By careful degrees she was able to move her head around on the pillow, taking in most of her surroundings.

This was not a typical log cabin. The roof rose to a peak in the center, where a metal chimney carried aloft smoke and cinders from the big central fireplace. The oddest thing, though, was the shape, and the lack of interior walls. The cabin's exterior walls defined five different living areas. Five sides . . . a pentagon. Like in Washington, D.C. Or like the basis for inscribing a pentagram, the shape used by witches and warlocks when casting their spells.

She didn't think the cabin had much in common with the Pentagon, no more than her host had in common with the regimented warriors and drones who peopled the Defense Department. He did, however, have something of the look of a warlock. Brooding and mysterious.

Somehow even that thought wasn't enough to disturb the inexplicable comfort she'd awoken with, a lazy sense of safety that she knew made no sense.

But then, she thought, watching Seth scrape the contents of a skillet onto a plate, her sorcerer had used his powers to save her, not to harm her.

Seth walked toward her, carrying a speckled blue plate that made her think of cowboys and camp fires. He set it, and the mug of coffee he held in his other hand, on the square table next to the bed. Then he turned away.

"Seth?" she said, when he went to a tall chest against the wall. "I, ah, I hate to bother you, but I don't think I can sit up without a little help."

He turned around, holding a blue shirt identical to the one he was wearing. "I'll help you sit up and get this on."

Get the shirt—oh, no. Tentatively she moved her leg and felt the sheet beneath, sheet and blankets above—all directly against her skin, nothing in between her and them, which meant . . . She moaned, grabbed the covers with one hand and pulled them up to her nose. That made her head hurt, so she squeezed her eyes shut.

A thread of humor laced his voice. "I think I'm the one who's supposed to close my eyes, not you."

He was amused? She opened her eyes and frowned.

If he'd been amused, he didn't look it now. His face was as impassive as ever, frustratingly so. And she was still naked, quite entirely naked, whether her eyes were open or closed. She sighed. "Do we know each other at all?"

"We do now."

"That's a lousy answer," she said, but she let go of the edge of the covers. There wasn't much point, was there? He'd undressed her and—oh, Lord! That horrible bedpan yesterday! If she'd been in any shape to pay attention, that should have clued her in to her lack of clothing. "I guess I'll need some help."

He sat on the bed beside her. With one arm he scooped her upper body off the bed. The covers fell to her waist. The movement made her head pound and her cheeks flush with embarrassment. She tried to help him get her arms into the sleeves, but she was so dratted weak, her efforts were probably more hindrance than help. When she looked down to button the shirt, she got dizzy and nearly toppled over, so he took over doing that, too.

She closed her eyes again. Illogical, maybe, but it gave her the illusion of privacy. It also left her oddly attuned to his scent, a unique blend of soap, coffee and male...to the movement of his hand...a sensation of warmth, the slight rasp of the cotton against her skin, her nipples, as he tugged button and buttonhole together...the careful way his hand shifted to avoid touching her breasts.

By the time he finished, her head pounded miserably. She was dizzy. And aroused.

She knew she should have felt embarrassed. He'd probably noticed her involuntary reaction to the intimacy of being dressed by his careful hands. But embarrassment, like fear, seemed like too much effort. So she just smiled at him when he settled her against the pillows he'd arranged to prop her up.

"Whew." Her heart thudded in rhythm with her head. "May I have some of that coffee now?"

He looked at her doubtfully, but whatever his objections, he didn't voice them.

He helped her hold the cup. The coffee was strong, dark and hot. His hand on top of hers, steadying the mug for a few sips, was strong and warm, too. He set the mug down and held the plate of eggs and buttered bread for her, but she managed the fork herself.

Apparently she wasn't a fussy eater. The overcooked eggs went down fine. At least a reasonable portion of them did—he'd given her enough to feed a fullback.

Once she persuaded him she really couldn't eat any more, he gave her three aspirins and made her drink half a glass of water before he'd let her have the few last sips of coffee.

"Thank you," she said, leaning back fully on the pillows. So many questions . . . they'd seeped in while she ate. "I have a lot to thank you for."

He didn't help her. Just sat there and watched her with his dark, dark eyes.

She licked her lips nervously. "How long have I been here?"

"Yesterday and last night. Part of the night before. I found you stumbling around Old Baldy in the middle of a storm."

"What's Old Baldy?"

"A mountain. Not especially high. Fifty years ago the top of it sheared off in an avalanche, so that today it looks bald. What do you remember?"

"You." And the bedpan. She bit her lip and glanced around. "I remember waking up in this room. Where are we?"

"The Davis Mountains, not far from McDonald Observatory."

"Near Fort Davis?"

He nodded.

She knew where that was. Texas. She felt a strong, diffused sense of relief. The knowledge carried a sense of familiarity. Fort Davis was in the far southwestern portion of the state, a desolate area half desert, half mountains. The Davis Mountains were the highest range in the area, high enough to wrest some rainfall from the thin, dry air.

They weren't gentle, though, these mountains. They were rugged and rocky, home to porcupines, skunks, rattlers and the occasional mountain lion. Storms here could be deadly, gorging the little creeks with floodwater . . .

. . . blinding her with a darkness that bled rain. Rocks sliding under her feet—falling, getting up, pushing on through a curtain of night and rain, and hurting, hurting from the fear as much as from the blow to her head—her head hurt so bad, so bad—

No, she thought. *No!* And as the nightmare faded away, so did the crippling pain in her head.

"... all right? Sophie?"

She opened eyes she didn't remember closing. Seth knelt by her bed, his hand on her shoulder.

"What?" she asked breathlessly. "What did you call me?"

"You had on a locket. That name is engraved on it." His dark eyebrows drew together in a frown. "It says, To Sophie on one side. With Love, on the other."

She wanted to react to the name, tried to find a feeling that went with it. But her momentary breathlessness was gone, leaving only exhaustion behind.

"Do you think that's your name?"

"I don't know. When I reach inside, I feel . . . like I'm stuffed with clouds instead of memories. You can't really touch clouds, can you? There's nothing there." Her eyes were so tired. "But you can call me Sophie. It was on the locket. Maybe—probably—it's my name."

"All right, Sophie. Go on back to sleep now. Everything will seem better when you're rested." His voice was a quiet, cool ribbon in the darkness behind her closed eyes, a ribbon she held on to gladly as she sank into the soothing blankness of sleep.

By the time Seth's patient woke up that afternoon it was drizzling again, and he was worrying.

Normally it didn't bother him when bad weather made the road to his cabin impassable. Even when the timing was unfortunate, like now, and he was low on propane or other supplies, he didn't mind being cut off from civilization.

But normally he didn't have an injured woman with beautiful breasts stretched out in his bed, wearing his shirt. Only his shirt.

Dammit, he did not need this. He liked silence. Solitude. He sure as hell did not want to be responsible for another human soul.

He glanced out the front door. Rocky lay on the porch, protected from the fresh drizzle. Being responsible for a dog was enough, more than enough. He didn't want the woman here.

But here she was, and neither of them had much choice about it. Seth sighed and looked at the book on the desk in front of him: *A History of Texas Wildlife.* Normally he enjoyed reading about his hobby, but today he couldn't concentrate.

He had a good view of his bed and its occupant from this desk. At least, he did if he turned his head to the right and looked through the crowded miscellany on the open shelves that divided the office from the sleeping area. So he noticed right away when she stirred, because he'd been looking that way a lot more than he'd been looking at the book he was supposedly reading.

Dammit. He wasn't going to go running in there just because she was moving around beneath those covers. If she needed anything, she'd call him. He wasn't going to...wasn't going to listen to himself, apparently, because he pushed his chair back and was already halfway there when she called him.

She lay in the bed and looked up at him. The scrapes on the left side of her face were scabbed over and ugly. She smiled. "Every time I wake up it smells good in here. Is that chicken soup?"

Why was she always smiling at him? He frowned, wanting her to stop. "I had to clean out the freezer. I'm too low on fuel to run the generator, so everything's defrosting and I need to use up what I can. I'll get you some."

"First things first." She tried to push up.

"Hey!" He got his arm behind her, bracing her. "You aren't ready for push-ups yet . . . Sophie."

She tipped her head, acknowledging his use of what might be her name. "Well," she said, her breath coming a little unsteadily, "I'll agree to wait on the push-ups, but I refuse to consider that bedpan again. There is a bathroom behind that door, isn't there?"

He nodded.

"Good." She smiled again. "But I might need a little help standing."

Good grief. Seth wasn't about to let the fool woman walk there. He disregarded her protests and carried her into the one area of the cabin separated from the rest by four walls and a door. He didn't like leaving her there, but agreed reluctantly when she agreed, with equal reluctance, to leave the door slightly ajar so he could hear her if she needed him.

Then he waited, scowling at the rocker and absently rubbing his thigh.

This is ridiculous, he told himself. She wasn't that special to look at. Different, yes. Pretty. Well, all right, more than pretty. She had incredible eyes. And her breasts—but he wasn't going to think about her breasts.

He knew about beautiful women, though, didn't he? He didn't miss that part of his other life. Sure, it had been awhile since a woman paid any attention to him, other than to look away fast. Two years and one month, or one year and nine months, depending on whether he counted from the accident or from his discharge from the hospital. But it was stupid for him to get flustered, to want to hang around her just to look at her. He hadn't acted like that around a female since he dated Cindy Grover in high school.

He knew better. Especially with a beautiful woman. Especially considering the white powder he'd found on her.

It wasn't as if she didn't notice his scars, either. She'd seen them first, just like everyone did. But she saw the rest of him, too, saw both sides of his face, not just the half the surgeon hadn't patched together all that well.

The thump from the bathroom nearly stopped his heart. "What the hell are you trying to do?" he demanded as he jerked the door open and saw her sitting on the platform that skirted the big sunken bathtub.

"I slipped when I sat down, that's all." The expression she faced him with was mule stubborn. "There's dried blood in my hair. I'm smelly. I have to take a bath."

Forget it, he started to say. But her expression told him he'd do better to outsmart her instead of arguing. "You can't do it yourself," he said. "I'll take your clothes off, lower you into the tub, and stay in here with you."

Her mouth opened. Closed. She looked at the deep, oversize tub he'd specially ordered when he was building the cabin. Then she proved him a fool. "Okay."

He should have known better. Seth pointed that out to himself as he filled the big tub while she waited, at his insistence, back in bed. Sweat trickled between his shoulder blades. He'd turned on the wall heater to get it warmed up in here for her. The amount of fuel it burned was negligible, after all. As for the fuel used to heat the water—well, he'd turn the hot water heater off again once her tub was ready.

He should have realized how contrary she'd be. She reminded him of the mare he'd owned years ago, back in high school. That mare had been a sweet-natured beast, affectionate and biddable. Every once in a while, though, she zigged when she was supposed to zag. That was how his collarbone got cracked the weekend before graduation.

He scowled at the faucet as he turned it off, then took his time rolling up his sleeves before testing the temperature of the water. Was it too hot? She was so soft. Delicate. How hot was too hot? Maybe he should let some of the water out, add more cold—

"Seth?" she called from the bed. "Is the water ready?"

The water was ready, he admitted silently. *He* wasn't ready, but he stood anyway. He'd better go get her before the stupid woman tried to hobble in here on her own.

She wasn't smiling at him now. In fact, she couldn't seem to get her gaze past the third button on his shirt when he stooped down and picked her up. "Listen," he said, "if you're having second thoughts—"

"No. No, I'm embarrassed, I'll admit, but I'm *dirty*, Seth. I have to have a bath." Shy as a butterfly, her glance lighted on his for a moment. "I trust you."

Well, now, that meant they were both fools, didn't it?

She was as perfect as he remembered. Exquisite, with her soft, white curves peeking out here and there as he unbuttoned the blue shirt. He tried not to look—tried, at least, not to get caught looking—while he helped her ease her incredibly naked body into the tub.

Her nipples weren't hard now, as they had been the first time he saw her breasts. Which was good, he told himself as he released her to the water. He must have gotten it warm enough in here for her to be comfortable. God knows his own temperature was nothing to judge by. It had shot up with the first button he'd unfastened while she sat there, docile and patient.

The little moan of satisfaction she gave as the warm water closed around her almost had him groaning, too. He turned away quickly. "There's soap and a washcloth on the ledge," he said gruffly. "Let me know if you need anything else."

She thanked him and started bathing. She made little splashing sounds, which had him picturing the way the water beaded on her bare skin. After a minute she started humming. It was a country tune. Well, he told himself, desperate for distraction, she was from Texas, judging by her accent and the way she'd recognized her location. Everyone in Texas knew some country songs, whether they—

A splash, too big and too loud, made him spin around.

She was all the way under the water.

Probably she would have been okay anyway. Probably. She hadn't knocked herself out again or anything, and was already pushing herself up when he got his arms around her and pulled her sopping body up against his chest.

"Dammit, woman." His heart galloped like that blasted mare had the day she refused the jump and broke his collarbone. "Dammit all. You're getting out right now." But he didn't move. Couldn't move.

"No, listen—" She pushed against him in the feeblest way. He managed to relax his hold a little. The face she tipped back to look at him was as pale as milk, like it had been when she was unconscious. The smile she tried on wouldn't stay put. "I'm all right. Really. I bent over to get my hair wet so I could wash it, and I got dizzy for a second. But it passed. I'm fine."

"Yeah, you're fine and I'm Little Boy Blue." He grunted as he shifted, needing to get his legs under him better before he lifted her. Kneeling like this made his thigh hurt.

"No—please!"

He paused. His shirt clung to his chest, wet with water from her very naked body. Her breasts—the breasts he'd been trying not to look at—just brushed his chest. His blood sang a hot, hot song.

"It's the blood," she said. "I can't stand having that dried blood in my hair any longer, Seth. Please."

This was a mistake. He was positive this was a mistake. So he was stern with her. "All right." She was getting some color back in her face already. That was good. "I'll wash your hair, though, not you. You took twenty years off my life when you went under like that. I won't let it happen again."

This wouldn't take long, he told himself. Her hair was already wet, so he just had to do the shampooing and then pour some water over her head to rinse. He dug around under the sink until he came up with an old mason jar to pour with.

Bracing her with an arm at her shoulders while he poured shampoo into the palm of his other hand was awkward. It brought him much too close to—well, to everything, all those warm, bare inches of her. Shoulders. Arms. Skin that looked even more delectable all wet, with little drops of water beaded on it, than he'd imagined it would.

"Seth? I can sit up."

Did she sound any different? Uncertain? She wasn't getting scared of him, was she? "Sure." He took a quick peek at her face, which was flushed. But the bathwater was pretty warm. No wonder she was flushed.

She was also very close. His soap definitely smelled different on her.

He cleared his throat. "I guess you can't tip over while I've got my hands in your hair," he agreed, and straightened enough to use both hands to lather the shampoo into her hair.

Mistake. Oh, yes, this was a huge, glaring, enormous mistake. He hadn't made one this large in years. He hurt. He was hard, and hurting, and he had to sound . . . normal. Unaffected.

"Almost done," he told her with dreadful, forced cheer. He urged her head back and poured water over her suds-slick head, water that ran down her back, glistening with soap bubbles. Quickly he rinsed again. He ran his fingers through her short, water-darkened curls to check for lingering soap, doing his best not to look below her forehead in front, but that left his gaze traveling down her back, down her straight spine to her narrow waist and on to the round cheeks of her bottom.

His skin was too tight and too hot. His thoughts thinned and his hands lingered rebelliously at their task as the rest of his blood went south to that most willful, demanding part of his body.

Her wet hair was silkier than that old mare's nose had been. Her eyes drifted closed and her lashes lay, long and pale, against the petal smoothness of her skin. Skin that was all pink and white, like blossoms. So pretty. Like her breasts, where the nipples now pointed out perkily.

Uh-oh.

His mouth opened as he stared at those hard little nipples. Sweat beaded on his forehead. He looked up.

Her eyes were open. They'd darkened from grass green to pure mystery. He heard her breath catch as their gazes locked. He reached out with one hand, brushing her cheek as gently as he knew how. "Don't be scared," he said. *Don't be frightened. I won't let my scars touch you when I kiss you now, when I touch that wonderfully soft, wet skin of yours and suck those perfect breasts and—*

Rocky's deep bark from directly behind him startled Seth so thoroughly he almost fell into the bathtub.

He pulled his hands back, clenching them into fists. Closed his eyes, and counted to ten. He'd been about to...very ready to...and his body still insisted on it, on the warmth and skin-to-skin closeness, and especially the part where he put himself inside a woman, inside this woman, and watched what happened to her shamrock eyes while he moved within her—

Rocky nudged his foot with her nose.

He opened his eyes.

Sophie hadn't moved. She sat in the cooling bathwater and stared at him with big, trusting eyes, her face still flushed with desire, looking as vulnerable as a new-hatched chick.

Which, he told himself with painful honesty, is what she was, in a sense. She didn't know who or what she was, had no memories to act as defense against the man-woman hunger that flared white-hot between them.

If, that is, she was telling the truth.

He thought she was. He didn't see how anyone could lie so convincingly while concussed. But amnesia, the sort of complete amnesia she claimed, was as rare as whooping cranes. Which was all the more reason for him to back off.

"That dog's always hungry these days," Seth growled as he grabbed the big towel he'd left on the ledge beside the tub. "Come on, get out before you catch a chill." He didn't actually lift her out. Didn't trust himself enough. Just slid his arm around her and held on while she got her legs under her. Together they got her sitting on the ledge again.

He promptly shrouded her in the big, blue towel. "How's that? Better?" Definitely better for him, with her all covered up like this. He started drying her hair with a second towel, which was another improvement. Now he couldn't see her at all. "Rocky's appetite is something these days. But then, she's probably eating for eight or ten, judging by the size of her stomach." He tried to wrap the towel around her head, turban style, so she wouldn't get chilled. "It looks as if those puppies are going to pop right out of her skin." Did he sound as stupid as he felt? He hadn't talked this much in months.

"Seth—"

"Ready to get back in bed? Hold on one more minute, and I'll have a clean shirt for you." How in the hell would he keep his hands off her while putting a shirt on her? How would he keep himself from learning the feel of those hard little nipples and the soft skin around them?

She touched his arm. "Seth?" Her hand was small and warm and much too welcome. Her eyes searched his—lovely eyes, a little eager, a little scared.

He made his expression harden. He couldn't afford to let her find whatever she was looking for in his face.

She glanced away, at the dog who'd plopped down beside him. "I didn't know you had a dog." She pushed the towel turban out of the way when it slipped down, and gave him a shaky smile. "It's all right. I know you're not going to ravish me or anything."

She sure as hell knew more than he did, then. "Come on," he said grimly. "Let's get you back in bed."

Seth was a bully. An oversize, gentle, worrywart of a bully. Sophie figured this out by the time he stuffed another pillow behind her and told her to behave and be still while he got her some more juice to drink with the supper she was finishing. He wouldn't let her get out of bed. He'd barely let her feed herself. He hadn't let her bathe herself...

Oh, but she couldn't regret that. She should, shouldn't she? She ought to be ashamed of the way she'd felt about having him look at her body—all hot and luscious, like melted fudge flowed in her veins instead of blood. Eager.

She wanted to feel that way again. Wanted him to look at her. Wanted . . . him. Was she the kind of woman who was casual with her body, then? The kind who, when she saw a man she wanted, thought that was reason enough for intimacy?

Or did she just want Seth?

He was back with her juice. "You haven't finished your soup."

"It's delicious, but my appetite is a little off."

He studied her, then took the almost empty bowl away. "All right. But you're looking tired," he said in his definite way. Bossy. "You need some more rest."

"I'm not sleepy, Seth. I've slept for most of the past forty-eight hours."

"You were unconscious for fifteen of those hours, and you get dizzy when you try to do anything. I'm no doctor, but that sounds like a concussion to me. You need to stay in bed."

She ignored the last statement. "What are you, then? You're not a doctor, but you seem to know what you're doing."

He hesitated, then set the bowl down. "I've had some paramedic training. These days, though, I'm a student." He tried to pull the covers up.

She swatted at his hand. "You are *not* tucking me in again. What are you studying? Medicine?"

"No. They don't offer medical degrees through correspondence courses."

Correspondence courses? "Yet you think you can boss me around." She tipped her head to one side, pleased when it didn't feel as if it were going to fall off. "I know. You're getting a degree from The Terminator School of Nursing, right?"

"No." But for all the terseness of his reply, his face relaxed. He was almost smiling.

Had she seen him smile? Since he rescued her and her memory started, had she once seen him really smile? She wanted suddenly, urgently, to know what he looked like when he was happy. "Ah," she said. "I've figured it out. You're embarrassed to admit it because you're a man, but you shouldn't be."

"What are you talking about?"

"Cooking." She gestured at the bowl on the table beside her. "You're taking cooking courses, and you've been practicing your lessons on me."

He shook his head. His hair swung loosely around his face, and she wondered if the scarred side was as sensitive as the other, if that skin felt the tickle of hair as acutely as unmarked skin. She wanted to find out. To touch him, and learn where he was sensitive . . .

His thin, cleanly shaped lips almost turned up. Almost. "Not cooking or nursing."

He liked being teased, she decided. He wasn't giving anything away, but he liked her teasing. The knowledge sang through her veins like a heady liquor. "Magic," she said softly.

He looked startled.

"I've figured out your secret. The five sides to your cabin give you away. You're a warlock, or at least you will be one when you graduate from Dr. Faust's Correspondence School of Magick. I'll be able to prove it," she added, "if I can find your gramarye."

"My grammar?" His lips twitched. "Do warlocks worry a lot about dangling participles, then?"

"Gram-ar-ee. You know, a magician's occult knowledge. A book of spells."

"Never heard of it."

"Ah, you must not read any fantasy."

"Do you?" he asked casually.

"I—" She stopped. Blinked, and fumbled mentally through the clouds that hid her memory, and came up with handfuls of fog. "I was going to say that I used to," she said slowly. "It was there for a minute, the knowledge that I used to read fantasy. But it's gone."

Thank goodness . . .

"But for a minute you knew," he said softly. "That proves your memory will come back." He supported her neck with one of his big, fascinating hands while the other urged her to lie back on the nest of pillows he'd built for her. "All you have to do is take it easy. Everything will come back in time."

He probably thinks he won that round, Sophie thought as Seth pulled the covers back up, his hands gentle, his face far too controlled. After all, she was lying down again, resting, like he wanted.

But that wasn't because of anything he'd done. Her own mind had distracted her after the glimpse of her past vanished back into whatever limbo it came from.

I was glad, she thought, bewildered, as Seth left on quiet feet. *I was glad I couldn't remember who I was.*

What was wrong with her? What kind of person was she? She craved a man she didn't know. And apparently she would prefer anything—or nothing—to reclaiming her own identity.

Three

In the morning after breakfast, Seth excused himself to go up on the roof and check out possible storm damage since, he said, the radio had reported the passing of the storm cell that had dumped all that rain on them. His guest managed not to comment on the foolishness of a man with a bad leg climbing around on the roof. At least he didn't seem to be limping today.

She took advantage of his absence to check something else out.

"Sophie." She said the name out loud, weighing it on her tongue. She smiled. "Sophie," she said again. A friendly name. Comfortable.

Her hand went to the delicate chain around her throat and the locket suspended there, with that name engraved in flowing script. She liked the feel of the dainty necklace, liked that one tangible link with her past.

Surely "Sophie" was a diminutive of some other, longer name. "Sophronia?" She had to smile at that one. Surely not. "Sophia," she tried, but the name sounded heavy and formal, and she couldn't summon any recognition.

She felt decidedly ambivalent about her name hunt. Part of her wanted to know. Part wanted to hide, wanted to lie here in Seth's bed where she felt safe and curiously free.

A loud clatter overhead recalled her to what she was supposed to be doing, and she started unbuttoning the shirt she'd slept in. Seth's trip to his roof gave her privacy to change into another of his shirts and the pair of panties that he'd washed out for her.

Why did she find the idea of Seth washing her panties more embarrassing than the idea of Seth washing her?

Sophie sighed as she drew the blue cotton down her arm. It was a nice arm, she thought. A little scrawny, maybe. Pausing with the shirt half off, half on, she made a muscle and giggled at her nonexistent biceps.

Apparently she was not into bodybuilding.

She glanced up. Continued sounds reassured her that Seth was still busy with his roof. In the bath last night she'd been so aware of Seth looking—or studiously not looking, at first—that she hadn't especially taken note of her body herself.

Sophie slipped the shirt all the way off and looked.

Her breasts were small. Her nipples were rather large, a sort of blushy tan color, but the breasts themselves were definitely on the small side. Oh, well. At least she wouldn't have to worry about sagging when she got older.

She frowned. Someone had said that to her. Someone, a woman quite a bit older, when Sophie was...was...but the thought trailed into a wisp. Vapor.

Maybe she was already "older." What an unsettling idea!

She stretched a leg out. She had pretty good muscle definition in her legs, she thought, but that didn't give her much of a clue as to her age. A dedicated runner or aerobics teacher might stay fit and firm well into her forties.

"I don't want to be forty," she muttered. She wasn't *supposed* to be forty. She was—well, she didn't know, but surely not forty.

She had to smile at herself. How absurd. She was more upset at the possibility of having passed her fortieth birthday than at her missing memories. Did she know on some level that she wasn't that old yet? Or was she feeling a purely human resentment at the passing of years?

She managed to squirm into her panties without making her head explode, and the bit of throbbing the movement excited eased off quickly. Pleased, she studied both legs.

Well, she thought, flexing one knee, she did have rather nice legs, whatever her age was. Her thighs were firm, and her calves . . . she ran a hand up from the ankle, and grimaced. Good muscle definition, but bristly. Maybe she could borrow Seth's razor later.

Or maybe she could borrow it now.

She glanced guiltily at the roof. She really shouldn't borrow his things without permission, but if she asked he'd probably insist on carrying her. She wasn't sure if the injury to his leg was temporary or permanent, but she didn't want his overly developed sense of chivalry making him hurt himself. Besides, she needed to be alone. It wasn't just a razor she wanted to find in the bathroom.

She needed a mirror.

She swung her legs off the bed. If she took it slow, she reasoned, walking to the bathroom shouldn't be too hard. Her head was much better today.

She scooted to the edge of the mattress and stood. The room moved.

It was a strange sensation. She clasped her hand to her head as if she could stop the slow gyrations of the room by clutching her head. Maybe it worked. After a moment, the world did steady itself and she started moving.

Her legs were mushy. Spaghetti al dente. She decided it would be wise to have something to hang on to, and swerved to take advantage of the furniture that lay between her and her goal. She paused to catch her breath, gripping the back of the couch where Seth had slept last night. Ridiculous to be all winded from such a tiny bit of exertion, but the room chose that moment to do its dance again. Black fluttered at the edges of her vision while the floor stood itself up on end and smacked itself against her outstretched hand, then knocked the breath from her lungs.

"Sophie!"

She didn't think she passed out again, but there didn't seem to be any time between hearing Seth cry out her name from the doorway and feeling him gather her up tenderly against him. Cursing her the whole time.

"...what the hell you thought you were doing? Of all the fool ideas—does that hurt?" He ran his hand up her legs. "You're a complete idiot, you know that?" He gently eased her head back against his shoulder to study her face intently. "Your pupils look the same," he muttered.

She wished he'd go back to touching her legs. The shivery sensation she'd had when his hands skimmed up her bare calves was fading. But this position had possibilities, too. His dark hair was tied back, emphasizing the elegance of the bones that underlay both sides of his face, the smooth and the damaged. His face was so near, with her head pillowed on his shoulder. He'd hardly have to move at all to...

To kiss her. Seth couldn't believe he was thinking about kissing her when one minute ago she'd nearly killed herself, toppling over just as he came inside. Lord, but he'd probably lost five years off his life. She'd scared him that badly. But right now her body was warm and soft against him and her lips were so near, gently rosy and curved up in that smile of hers, as if she knew what he was thinking and liked it, liked the idea of his mouth on hers. Her eyes had the slumberous look of a woman who wanted a man.

The thought that she might actually want him jolted through his body, making him instantly hard and throbbing.

Her hand crept beneath his hair to the back of his neck, where her fingertips skimmed a hesitant circle.

His body responded to the uncertain caress with pure, ravenous hunger. "Good Lord," he breathed, and jerked back.

She blinked, but if his sudden rejection stung it didn't show. Unless the huskiness in her voice came from hurt feelings instead of arousal. "That was really weird," she said. "The room went haywire on me all of a sudden."

"Try 'stupid' instead of 'weird.'" He shifted her so he could stand. "Didn't you know I would help you if you needed to use the bathroom?" He interrupted his scolding to grunt as he stood, bringing her up with him.

"Oh, Seth, don't. Your leg—"

Great. She'd noticed him limping. "It's fine. Now, do you need to go to the bathroom?"

She ignored his question. "I'm fine, too. Or almost fine, anyway. I can walk. You might have to help me a bit, but I can walk."

He obviously shouldn't have given in to her pleas that morning to be allowed to make it into the bathroom on her own two feet. It had given her delusions of health. "You are one damn fool woman. Now which do you want—back to bed, or to the bathroom?"

She sighed. "Bed."

Sitting with her on the bed was easier on his knee than bending to lay her down. He certainly didn't do it because the trusting warmth of her body, or the arms she'd wrapped around his neck as he carried her, were already dear to him. Desire was understandable. Predictable, under the circumstances. "Dear" was—well, ridiculous.

"Why were you up?" he asked, scowling. She sat right up against his thigh, much too close. He'd have to move, in just a second. "If you didn't need the bathroom, why were you heading that way?"

Her teeth gnawed on her lower lip. She looked away. "I wanted to borrow your razor."

He stared. "You wanted to *what?*" He couldn't believe it, couldn't believe she'd risked herself over something so trivial. "How could you be so stupid? And if you absolutely had to shave your legs, why didn't you wait until I came back in so I could help you?"

"Because I didn't want you to help me! Because—" Now she turned her face to him. Her eyes glistened like rain-soaked grass. "Because I wanted to find a mirror. I don't know what I look like, Seth, and I wanted—I wanted to be by myself when I found out. I don't know why."

Oh, Lord. He ran his hand through his hair.

She didn't know what she looked like. What an idiot he was, not to have realized she'd need to see her face. "There's no mirror in the bathroom."

"But when you shave—"

"I don't need a mirror to shave." He didn't need to look at her, either, when he talked to her. So he didn't. "There's a mirror in the pickup. I'll take you out there. But I'll let you be alone to look. I won't intrude."

"Seth," she said, sounding as if she was about to cry. He felt like more of a fool than ever. He should have anticipated this. "Oh, Seth," she said again, "do your scars bother you that much?"

His gaze jerked back to her.

Her lips trembled into a smile. "I'm sorry. I guess you don't like to discuss it, but learning that you don't have a mirror in your house, well..." She lifted her hand and touched him on the left side of his face.

He couldn't move. He tried, he could have sworn he tried to move, but her fingers were kitten-soft. Then she moved. Drew closer. And brushed her lips across his cheek in a gentle kiss.

He carried her out to the pickup. As they crossed the porch, Rocky sighed a gusty canine sigh and heaved herself to her feet. She'd assigned herself two jobs when she moved in with Seth last month: chasing deer and rabbits away from

his gardens, and accompanying him whenever he went outside. She obviously didn't consider advanced pregnancy
reason enough to shirk her duties.

Sophie gave him a hard time. She wanted to walk, but he
pointed out how muddy the ground was, how she might slip,
and how he was already carrying her and had no intention
of putting her down, so she might as well quit being so bossy
and relax.

"Me, bossy? You've got to be kidding. You're the one
who's studying with the Terminator School of Nursing."

She went on to explain to him exactly how bossy he was
as he and the dog skirted the biggest puddle, and he nodded agreeably. Her fingers still clutched at his shirt too
tightly, but the hint of panic fluttering around behind her
eyes had eased off as soon as she started arguing.

He knew just how frightening it could be, having to face
your image in a mirror for the first time. Of course, her situation wasn't like his had been, but the fear might be similar.

He opened the pickup's door and slid her onto the seat.
"It's dirty," he said apologetically. "I use it to haul stuff."

"That doesn't matter." Her tone was as absent as her
straight-ahead gaze, and she still clutched his shirt.

"I'll let you be alone now," he said, and patted her hand
to remind her that he couldn't leave until she turned him
loose.

"I've changed my mind," she said suddenly.

He waited.

"I don't want you to leave me alone." She looked at him.
"Stay with me?"

In answer he gently scooted her over and sat down behind the steering wheel.

She took a deep breath, reached for the rearview mirror
and angled it toward her.

Seth tried not to watch her. She might have changed her
mind about doing this alone, but that didn't mean she
wanted to be stared at. He bent and scratched Rocky be-

hind the ears, and he waited. But Sophie was quiet for so long he had to look.

She held her head tipped so she could study the left side of her face, where the scabbed-over scratches made ugly tracks. Her fingers traced those scabs anxiously.

"They're pretty shallow," he said gently. "It may take them awhile to fade completely, but they shouldn't scar."

Her head jerked toward him. "Seth, I didn't mean to—"

"No one wants to be scarred. Especially not a beautiful woman."

Her eyebrows went up in two surprised half circles as if she didn't believe him when he called her beautiful. She shook her head slightly and looked back into the mirror. "I don't think I'm forty yet, do you?"

"I don't think you're thirty yet," he said dryly.

She sighed. "I guess I'm finished staring at myself."

She was quiet while he carried her back inside, not chattering and smiling. He was sure he liked it better that way. If she'd stay quiet he could pretend she wasn't here.

When he bent to set her back in the bed, her arms tightened around his neck briefly. And she did it again. Kissed him, right on his scarred cheek.

"Thank you, Seth," she whispered, and turned him loose.

The next day Seth still felt that kiss. Both kisses.

Bright, blue-lit skies shone down on the scrub oaks that staggered up the slopes surrounding his small valley and the cabin he'd built after leaving the hospital almost two years ago. The radio weatherman said another front was moving in, but it was supposed to miss this area. The skies should be clear for days.

Sophie rebelled.

He'd managed to ignore her yesterday by working in the south garden and the drying shed for hours, something he'd needed to do anyway if he didn't want his harvest to date of seeds to go to waste. She'd pestered him with questions last night. Not that he'd minded telling her about his gardens. They weren't that big a deal, after all. The world wouldn't be a different place if he did manage to breed a commercially useful Mexican persimmon. So what if he'd taken a few courses? It was just a hobby, like he told her.

Apparently Sophie had no intention of letting him ignore her that way today. The sun was bright, the sky was blue, and she wanted out.

At lunchtime Seth gave in. The blasted woman wasn't going to stay still and rest, and he couldn't have her scaring him again like she had yesterday. So he helped her out onto the porch, where they had sandwiches.

Of course, after they finished eating, she was still convinced she wasn't sleepy.

Rocky lay on her scrap of blanket at the south end of the porch. Seth sat on one side of the old table he'd found in an abandoned shack near Ridgemore last year. Sophie sat on the other side in the big rocker he'd brought out for her, a pillow beneath her bottom and a smaller one behind her head. A quilt covered her legs, at his insistence. The scabbed-over stripes on her cheek faced him when she glanced at Rocky. This afternoon she wasn't smiling at Seth. She was grinning.

And winning. "Gin," she said, laying her cards down on the weathered table, where she had been trouncing Seth at cards for the past two hours.

Fool woman, getting all excited about a game of cards. He made a disgusted noise. "You're an obnoxious winner. I should have insisted on Scrabble."

"You didn't want to take advantage of me," she said smugly. "I have a head injury, after all. Scrabble might be too hard on me." She tipped her head, trying to see the scores he was adding up. Sunlight tangled in the different shades of blond in her hair. "How much do you owe me now?"

"Sixty-seven thousand, five hundred dollars," he said dryly. "But wait until you see the medical bill I'm sending you. I hope your insurance is paid up."

"No problem." Her smile tilted some before she got it straightened. "We've agreed I'm rolling in money, right? My clothes, my watch, all my possessions look pretty high dollar." Her hand went to her throat, where the locket gleamed, golden. "Even if my insurance isn't paid up, I'll take care of my debts."

Maybe she wasn't as unfazed by her lack of memory as she seemed. She kept touching that locket. "I've got a clumsy tongue, haven't I?"

"You can't watch every word you say. Almost everything, I'm learning, has ends trailing back into the past." She patted the cards into a neat stack. "My deal."

"It's been your deal since you grabbed that deck of cards out of my hand."

"Yeah," she said, her slow smile striking sparks in her green eyes. "But you'll go on humoring me, because I'm convalescing." She shuffled the cards, bridging their corners between her busy hands like a card shark, and began dealing. "I've been meaning to ask you about those big sticks you've stuck in the ground over there." A bob of her head indicated the construction he'd begun on the level ground roughly south of the cabin.

"Sticks? Are you talking about those trimmed ten-inch logs?" He picked up his hand and spread the cards. Another bust, looked like.

"To me, they're logs. I figured that, big as you are, you'd call them sticks." Her eyes smiled at him over the tops of her cards. "What did you do, get bored one afternoon and play javelin toss with them? If so, your aim is off. There are a bunch more lying on the ground than are stuck in it."

The little imp was flirting with him. Which was flat-out stupid, under the circumstances. "It's a stable," he said curtly, closing up his face and his feelings. "Or it will be.

The logs on the ground will have to stay there until my cousins come down for a weekend again.''

''I see.'' Her eyes drooped down to her cards, which she studied so long, so silently, Seth wanted to cut his tongue out.

But he couldn't let her tease him. Not when her eyes smiled like that and made the delicate skin beneath them, where shadows still lurked, crinkle up happily. Not when her comment on his size made him feel powerful, and his body reacted in a thoroughly male way to her appreciation. Especially not when all he could think about was that yesterday she would have let him kiss her.

What else would she have let him do?

''So,'' she said, drawing and making her discard at last. ''You must like horses.''

He shook his head, more at his own stupidity than in response to her statement. ''Not really.''

She tipped her head to one side, and her smile, God help him, was edging back. ''I see. You just like building stables.''

He almost smiled back. Almost. ''No one who knows horses ought to admit to liking them. Not unless he's been kicked in the head a time too many. The fool beasts average half a ton or better of pure orneriness. They're skittish, stubborn and unpredictable. I have a theory,'' he said, picking up the king she'd tossed, ''that God gave us horses after we stirred up trouble back in that garden to remind us that temptation has consequences.''

Her mouth reminded him of temptation, even when she held it all prim like that. Her eyes laughed at him. ''So what will you put in your stable?''

''Horses, of course. I like riding, and they are pretty much the only option. Camels are too mean, elephants too big. You can put a saddle on a cow, but it's just not the same.''

She laughed out loud. The sound swept through him like a spring breeze, lifting dust in unused corners of his soul.

"And," she said, leaning forward, "if you put a saddle on a male cow, called a bull in some circles, you're in danger of getting the stuffing knocked out of you. I always used to go get something from the concession stand when the bull-riding portion of the rodeo came along."

"Did you?" he asked, struggling to keep from jumping up and grabbing her. Did she realize what she had just said? "A little squeamish about the sight of blood, are you?"

"I..." She stopped with her mouth open. All the color drained from her face.

Sophie sank back against the rocker's slatted back. The pillow slipped and she felt hard wood behind her head. She also felt Seth's hands close around her arms, but for a time she didn't see, didn't hear, anything from the present. A terrible isolation blinded her. Biting, bitter grief mixed with guilt and rain. Not a storm. An endless drizzling rain falling on a Houston cemetery. She saw the subdued colors of the women's clothes and the black and navy suits worn by the men. Umbrellas sprouted over everyone's heads like dripping mushrooms. She saw gray headstones and the wound in the ground where they were about to lower her sister and it was her fault, her fault—

She made a sound, a choked-off gasp, and she heard it and came back.

Seth's big shoulders filled her vision. His hands moved. He was about to pick her up. "No!" She pushed weakly at him. She couldn't stand for him to touch her, couldn't stand him to see, to know. "Seth," she said as he drew back. "Seth, my sister's dead."

He didn't say anything. His face was still close to hers and his eyes, dark and shiny and near, reflected her pain and his worry.

"Oh, God," she said, and closed her eyes.

She felt his withdrawal. Knew it inside her as much as she heard it in the rustle of cloth as he retreated, giving her the space he somehow realized she needed. Her fingers were cramping from her grip on the chair's arms. Inhaling slowly, she eased her hands loose.

"You've remembered?"

"No." Her denial was sharp, as if one word could cut her free from what lay on the other side of the fog in her mind. "Not much, just that...I had a sister, and she's dead." She forced herself to open her eyes. "And it was my fault."

Seth crouched near her chair, waiting with unblinking intensity. His silence pulled more words from her. "I saw her grave. It was raining, and we were in the Ridgehill Cemetery in Houston. I think—I think maybe Houston is where I live. It seemed very familiar. But that's all I brought back with me. No names, just an image of her funeral, and..." Guilt. A suffocating weight of guilt. "That's all I remember," she repeated. "The rest is gone."

Seth remained still, his eyes never leaving her face. She didn't know why his silent study didn't bother her, why, in fact, she felt safer, somehow, under the watchful regard of those dark eyes. Finally he spoke. "I don't think your memory loss is physical, do you?"

She stiffened. "You mean I've just been imagining this headache?"

"Probably the original disorientation came from your injury. But now, I think, you don't remember because you don't want to remember."

She looked away. Tried to will him away.

She heard the movement as he stood, and the scrape of the chair when he brought it over and set it close to her rocker. She refused to look at him.

"I could be wrong," he said. "It happens. But most cases of complete retrograde amnesia like you've got are hysterical in nature. That doesn't mean the victim runs around screaming and crying. In medical terms, 'hysterical' means there are real, troublesome symptoms involved that don't have a physical cause."

"You think I'm making all this up," she said flatly. "That I'm nuts."

"You're not crazy. You've lost some of your connections, though. You feel like you've got clouds in your head where your memories should be. Now you tell me that your sister is dead, that you feel responsible, and you can't remember anything else. It sounds like you're afraid to remember."

A hand, one of Seth's big hands, touched her arm. She felt the heat from his palm, the strength in his long, capable fingers as they gently curved around her arm. "Maybe I won't like the person I am—or was," she whispered.

"Maybe." He paused. "But I don't think you'll find that you're such a bad person. Shall I tell you what I've figured out about you?"

She reached for the locket at her throat. Rubbing her thumb over the engraving soothed her. "I'd rather leave the subject alone for now."

He'd asked, but he sure didn't pay attention to her answer. "The way you've acted with me right from the start tells me you're much too trusting, in the way that fundamentally honest people tend to be. Maybe that's why you think you should be tough, which you aren't, except on yourself. You push yourself too hard. Oh, and you don't take orders worth a damn." One end of his mouth turned up, as if he were encouraging her to find her smile again.

He'd embarrassed her, but it was a nice sort of embarrassment. "All right, Sherlock. What else have you figured out? Anything more concrete?"

"You're Texan," he answered promptly. "About five foot five, one hundred ten pounds. Right-handed. Green eyes, naturally blond hair, and between twenty-four and twenty-eight years old. Based on the outfit you were wearing, I'd say you're probably well-off, and you prefer the subtlety of texture and style in your clothes to the flash of sequins."

"So I'm young, blond and tastefully rich. A society girl. Sounds like a great life, if you like being a decoration."

"Being wealthy doesn't automatically make you fluff."

"You don't have any evidence otherwise."

"Sure I do. You're a runner, which isn't a country club sport the wealthy pursue automatically. It demands discipline. And before you ask—yes, I do have evidence. Those shoes you had on didn't go with your outfit, but they were well worn and obviously yours, from the fit. Also, you're, uh, you're in very good shape." His gaze skittered away from hers, and he turned his head away. A strand of hair that had come loose from the leather thong swung gently with the motion.

He was embarrassed? She was the one who should be bothered about all he'd seen of her. But she wasn't. She wanted to touch that loose strand of hair, tuck it back behind his ear.

"Then," he said, getting his eyes straightforward once more, "there's your choice of reading material. It seems significant that you know fantasy so well that it was the first thing you remembered about yourself."

"I can't imagine why."

"No? Think about it. Fantasy is always about the struggle between good and evil, the triumph of good over evil." He smiled suddenly. "Morally bankrupt people do not concern themselves much with good and evil."

She stared. She'd been right—Seth's smile transformed him the way the sun, emerging from the troubled darkness of storm clouds, transforms a bleak day.

His smile reached inside and transformed something in her, too. For a moment she believed wholly, blindingly, in the power of the sun. She stretched out her hand slowly. Wanting to touch him the way he'd touched her.

His smile evaporated. He leaned back in his chair, away from her.

Her hand fell to her lap. *It's not me,* she told herself fiercely. *He's not rejecting me, just the idea of touching.* He didn't necessarily think she was bad or unworthy or any of the things she was so afraid she was.

His voice, clipped and neutral, matched his expression. "What you weren't wearing when I found you is significant, too. No wedding ring."

"Maybe I took it off." She dared him, with a look, to argue. To make her be wrong. "Maybe I like to cruise the bars, see what I can pick up."

"Look." He grabbed her hand and held it up in front of both of them. "You see? Your hands have a faint tan. There's no white mark left from where a ring would go." He dropped her hand.

She let out a breath she hadn't noticed she was holding and, with a push from her toes, started the rocker moving. He had tried so hard—and against his natural reticence—to make her feel better about herself. She had to give something back.

Play, she decided. He needed to play. "You're pretty good at this deduction stuff, you know that? But now it's my turn. You," she said firmly as she rocked, "were the oldest of six children, and you bossed all your younger siblings around."

A hint of something, maybe humor, moved in his dark eyes. "I was an only child."

"Impossible. Only the oldest brother would develop your particular, irritating mixture of responsibility and pure bossiness."

The corner of his mouth turned up on the undamaged side. "Maybe you're right. Do cousins count?"

"Definitely." A tingling exhilaration pierced her. Was he actually going to tell her something about himself?

"I was raised with my two cousins after my parents died." His dark, watchful eyes waited for her reaction.

She kept rocking gently. Kept her voice light, deliberately. "There, you see? You learned how to be a tyrant from an early age."

"My cousins are both older than me."

She frowned at him for trying to trick her. "Amazing. It's very unusual for the youngest child to be able to boss the others around."

The gleam in his eyes was definitely humor. "Did I mention when I was listing your qualities that you hate to admit it when you're wrong?"

"Nope. Did I mention that you have a sly, sneaky streak that could get you in trouble?"

For over an hour, rocking and teasing gently, Sophie coaxed bits of Seth's story from him. It was like pulling—well, not teeth, she decided. Taffy? Because the few facts she managed to draw from him stuck to her like that gooey homemade candy, blistering in places the way taffy does if you start pulling it before it's cool enough.

Like her, Seth had lived in Houston, though he'd spent the first part of his childhood in the hard, wild country around Alpine and Fort Davis. He talked about the city, and about the aunt and uncle who'd raised him and still lived there. The cousins he'd been raised with, Tom and Raz, were both police officers like Seth's uncle had been before his retirement.

Sophie wasn't sure what to think about those cousins. They'd helped Seth build his cabin. They came to see him every so often. Yet she heard a distance in his voice when he referred to them, and she wanted badly to know whether that distance was their doing or Seth's.

Because she knew better than to ask, she let him change the subject to Rocky, his very ugly, very pregnant dog, and how she'd shown up on his doorstep one day.

Kind of like me, Sophie thought.

He didn't mention his accident or his scars. He didn't refer to any people in his life other than his cousins. Except for one.

Her name was Linda, and she had mattered. He'd been talking about Houston when he said her name in connection with a play he'd seen, and a silence fell behind his eyes. So Sophie knew Linda had been important, and that she had hurt Seth. Sophie didn't much like the way that knowledge made her feel, but she accepted it, just as she accepted that this man with two faces—one closed and forbidding, the other gentle, wry, and inexcusably caring—mattered to her.

A lot.

Seth loved these rough mountains, that was clear. Much of the land in the Davis Mountains was privately owned, he said, and most of the landowners were conscious of the need to protect and preserve. "Conservation has been around a long time," he told her. "Long before environmental concern became politically correct, people around here paid attention to the land." He fell silent, looking out across the little valley that held his cabin.

She rocked, not minding the silence. Somewhere a bird scolded. "I think I must have been a city girl," she said at last. "I don't know the names for anything—the birds or the plants. But I like it here. I like it a lot."

They sat in companionable quiet a few more moments. Then he stood, slowly. Maybe reluctantly. She wanted to think he was as reluctant to end the sharing as she was for him to end it. "I'd better take a run up the road, see if it's dry enough to travel yet. But first..." He moved so close to her chair she had to tilt her head back to see him. Then he bent.

His lips startled hers—one brief blaze, gone almost before it happened. She stared, astonished. His eyes—why couldn't she read what she needed to know in his eyes, when they were so full of meanings?

"Thank you," he said, straightening.

Sophie stared at Seth as he swung down from the porch and crossed the yard to his mud-splattered pickup with the jacked-up chassis and big tires. He got in, started it and drove off down the twin ruts that passed for a road. She watched until he rounded the bend that followed the slope of the mountain, taking him out of sight.

Why had he thanked her? For the kiss? For listening?

Maybe. Seth, Sophie was starting to understand, was a lonely man. Strongly independent and capable of withstanding that loneliness, yes. But still very much alone. He lived at the end of a dirt road in some of the most rugged and underpopulated country in the state, in the whole country. He didn't even have a phone to connect him to the rest of the world.

Seth wasn't gone long, maybe twenty minutes. When he returned he was pleasant in his grave way, and went straight inside to start supper. Sophie stayed outside, rocking, listening to the chiding of some unseen bird. *Tut-tut, tut-tut.* High up in the clear mountain sky a hawk circled lazily. She watched the early evening shadows stretch across the ground, and felt again the touch of his lips on hers. His mouth had closed a connection inside her, leaving a light burning in a place that had been waiting for him so long.

So long. Even without memories, she knew that. Felt it. She rocked gently and thought about his kiss and his watchfulness and his big, careful hands, and wondered if what she wanted was wrong. Her instincts said that Seth was absolutely right for her, but how could she trust her instincts, when she didn't know what kind of person she was?

And even that wasn't the most important question. What really mattered was whether she would be any good for Seth, and she was afraid she knew the answer to that.

Four

Seth stood at the sink finishing up the supper dishes. He shook his head at himself. Earlier he'd talked his fool head off. Then, just to prove he was an idiot, he'd kissed her.

"What's a seven-letter word meaning 'to bear up against and come safely through'?" Sophie asked. She sat at the polished oak table Seth had made last year after finishing the cabin. A crossword puzzle book lay open in front of her, and one of the kerosene lanterns cast its mellow glow over them both.

"You know any of the letters?"

"It starts with a *w* or a *t.*"

He drew a blank. "I'll have to get back to you on that one," he said, pulling the plug to let the dishwater drain.

She muttered something he didn't catch, then fell silent again.

The kiss had been a mistake. Seth recognized that, accepted it. Not for the reason he'd expected. She hadn't cringed away from him. No, she'd accepted his lips with wide-eyed astonishment. And pleasure. He'd seen the pleasure in her eyes, in her faintly pink cheeks. But still, the kiss was a mistake.

He wasn't too arrogant to admit it when he was wrong. Not anymore. So he was very aware of the possibility of making a much worse mistake with Sophie. Aside from the obvious stupidity of getting involved with a woman who didn't even know whether or not she was married, it would be wrong to take advantage of her dependency on him.

Thank God it was just lust. As long as he remembered that, he'd be okay. Sure, he wanted her, but that was no surprise. She was beautiful, needy, and reacted to him as if he'd never lost half his face when a ball of smoke and gas ignited and the air itself burned him. So he was susceptible. He wouldn't let himself pretend it was anything more when he really didn't know a thing about her.

Except that he could no longer believe the white powder meant what it seemed to mean.

"Weather!" she said.

"What?"

"The word I was looking for that means 'to bear up against and come safely through.' It's *weather.* Now, what's a four-letter word for firmness of character?"

He thought while he dried the skillet. *"Grit."*

"Oh. That fits."

Seth put the pan up and paused, trying to find something more to do to delay turning around and seeing her. His work shirt was too large for her, and the last time he'd turned around she'd been leaning over the table to work on her crossword puzzle. His view had been breathtaking.

On two other nights he'd seen more of the soft mounds of her breasts than the shirt revealed, of course. Maybe that was the problem. He remembered exactly what it was he couldn't quite see.

"How about a six-letter word, starting with *s,* and ending with *o-p-h-i-e,* for a useless parasite?"

He turned, fighting the smile that tugged at his lips. "You're not a parasite, you're injured."

"I feel pretty useless." She shrugged one shoulder, sending the shirt slipping crookedly. "I'm much better now, Seth. You needn't act like I'll keel over if I stand up for a minute or two. I could have dried while you washed."

"Oh, yeah?" The smile was winning. She was so determined. Foolishly, of course, since she was far from recovered. "The other word fit you better, you know."

She blinked.

"Grit," he said, pulling the dish towel from his waist and setting it on the counter. "That describes you pretty well."

"Let's not talk about me, okay? It leaves me without much to contribute."

He'd thought hard about this, and didn't like his decision much better than he figured she was going to. "I'm afraid we have to." He joined her at the table, but didn't sit. "About your situation, Sophie—"

"I'm starting to remember," she interrupted, leaning forward. "Twice now I've recalled bits from my—my other life. Let's just wait awhile, Seth, and let it come back at its own pace."

The hope in her face hurt him. Slowly he shook his head.

She turned away, presenting him with a view of her disorderly blond hair and the scrapes on her left side. "All right." She threw up one hand. "All right! I suppose we should turn me and my troubles over to some authority somewhere. They'll fingerprint me, and voilà! I have an identity again."

"It doesn't work that way. The FBI keeps a pretty extensive file of fingerprints, but those prints belong to armed forces personnel, convicted felons, and certain government employees. Chances are you don't fall into any of those categories. But we do need to decide whether to contact the sheriff. You probably have family who are desperately worried by now."

"I don't think so." She rubbed at a whorl of wood on the table without looking up. "Surely I'd feel it somehow if there was someone."

"Not necessarily. Sophie..." *Get it said,* he told himself. "When I left today to check out the road I went to a pay phone. I talked with my cousin Raz in Houston. I wanted him to check into things at his end before we contact the sheriff here." Her eyes were big with what he thought was distress. "Raz is okay," he assured her, resting one hand on her shoulder. "He and Tom are two of the good guys." He knew he could count on them. They'd more than proved that in the past two years.

"You could have discussed it with me first!" She knocked his hand away. "Even if I don't remember, it's still my life! Look," she said, lifting one hand and opening it. She flexed her fingers, inspecting them. "I feel a sort of fond recognition when I look at my hand, and yet I don't know if I bit my nails in junior high, or whether I've ever worn an engagement ring on the third finger. But it's still mine."

She relaxed her hands and looked up at him. "You're right. There are a lot of questions that need answers, even if I don't like the answers. Like whether someone tried to kill me the other night, and whether I might be safer if no one knew I was here with you. That's what you mean by my 'situation,' isn't it, Seth?" An unhappy smile twisted her mouth. "You didn't think I'd considered it at all, did you?" Abruptly she shoved her chair back and stood.

He got up, reaching for her. "Sophie, come back and sit—"

"No! No, dammit, I do not want to sit and rest and be sensible." She paced away, then spun, arms outstretched. "See? I didn't fall over."

No, she hadn't. But her face was almost as pale as that first night. "We don't know for certain that anyone's trying to harm you." His arms hung helplessly at his sides.

"But it's a possibility, isn't it? I showed up on your mountain in the middle of a storm, wearing evening clothes

and running shoes—a pretty odd fashion statement—and
obviously running from something. Or someone."

She started to pace. "I have thought about this, Seth. I
couldn't get to sleep last night, so I made myself put together the possibilities. And I only come up with two. I either got hurt accidentally, or on purpose. Maybe I had an
accident on that highway you said lies on the other side of
Old Baldy, and wandered off into the storm. Pretty stupid
on my part, but I could've been dazed or something. Or
maybe I was running from someone who hurt me. Someone who might want to finish the job."

Reluctantly he spoke. "I've been listening to the news
regularly on the radio. There's been no mention of a
wrecked car with a missing driver."

She paused between the table and the hearth, where a low
fire painted fitful shadows over her down-turned face and
her long, creamy legs. "Would there be? I mean, even in a
rural area like this, surely they don't mention every abandoned car on the radio."

"A vehicle that's been in a wreck in the middle of a bad
storm, then abandoned—yes, it would have been mentioned on the news, because they would have called out the
search-and-rescue people to look for the driver. If your car
had been found." The conclusion was inescapable. He'd
reached it himself when he realized that he had to force this
discussion.

"So." She stared into the fire for long moments. "We're
left with the other alternative, then. But why didn't you
want to contact your sheriff about me? Are you not sure if
we should trust him?"

We. The word settled into Seth's guts with all the subtlety of a knife—sharp and significant. He couldn't trust it.
"As far as I know, Sheriff Reed is an honest, experienced
lawman."

"Then—oh, no." Her hand stretched out to ward him off,
though he hadn't moved. "You think I was running from
the police. That I'm some kind of criminal."

Seth had known he would hate this. He hadn't realized he'd feel like her judge, jury and executioner. But he made himself go over to the corner cabinet in the kitchen and remove the object he'd left in the biggest serving bowl. He came back and laid the small plastic bag of white powder on the table.

She stared at it. Her eyes lifted to his.

"It was in your pocket," he said.

She went to the table. She sat, slowly, in the chair she'd bolted from earlier. Clasped her hands on the table in front of her, not touching the bag he'd set there. All at once her face crumpled. "Oh, God."

He remained stupidly, stubbornly, where he was. He didn't know whether willpower or cowardice kept him from going to her. Maybe both.

She covered her face with her hands, but she didn't cry. Didn't move. Her voice, when she spoke, was supremely level. "It's cocaine, isn't it?"

He hadn't known until this moment how much he'd wanted, needed, her to convince him of her innocence. "I don't know. It seemed foolish to try tasting it or something when I'm not sure what I'd be putting in my mouth, or what cocaine tastes like, for that matter."

A log settled with a small thump in the fire pit. She pulled her hands away from her face and stared at them. Her chest rose and fell in a long, soundless sigh. "I suppose it might be heroin. Isn't heroin a powder at one stage of its processing?"

"I think so."

Suddenly she shoved at one of her sleeves, pushing it up past her elbow, twisting her arm to peer at the veins.

"There aren't any needle marks." He had to move. Had to. "And you haven't gone through withdrawal." He lost the battle to hold himself apart and started toward her.

She looked up, her eyes wild in the reddish fire glow. "You checked for needle tracks, did you? But most coke users sniff their poison instead of injecting it, so you wouldn't find anything. And cocaine isn't physically addictive, so no withdrawal."

"Coke users develop runny noses, watery eyes, and you don't—"

"So I'm a short-timer. Or maybe I just sell the stuff. Maybe—"

"Stop it!" He bent and seized her shoulders, turning her in her chair to face him. "You're not a seller. You're not a user."

"But I feel guilty," she whispered. "When I look at that bag I feel guilty."

Seth's hands were still on her shoulders. He pulled her up, and she came, her gaze fixed on his. He hated the expression on her face. So he pulled her to him and tucked her head against his shoulder.

She was stiff. For three or four long seconds her body refused his solace, then her resistance ebbed like a tide going out. Her body relaxed and softened into his, while his hardened. *Maybe she won't notice.* Her arms slipped around his waist. Her breath was warm against his chest. He felt each exhalation distinctly through the worn cotton of his shirt. His head bent, and tentatively he rubbed his undamaged cheek against her hair.

Soft. Good. *Oh, Lord,* he thought, closing his eyes. *Being a fool feels wonderful.* "For all we know," he told her, "you're a narcotics officer. Or DEA. There are a lot of explanations for that bag being in your possession."

"An undercover cop?" She considered it, unmoving. "But if I were undercover, then those clothes I had—the locket, everything—would be part of my cover. Not me. And I—I've gotten used to thinking of myself as Sophie."

When she pulled away she seemed to draw something out of him, some essential part of him that went with her. But she only pulled back far enough to search his face. Her hands still touched him. His arms still closed loosely around her. "You thought I was guilty," she said, very low. "Your face doesn't give away much, but I could tell what you thought when you showed me that bag."

"I didn't know." *I still don't.* "But when you saw that powder, you seemed to recognize it."

"Then why did you say I'm not a user or a dealer?"

Because she smiled at him. Because her hair felt so soft against his cheek, and he'd seen the beauty of her nakedness and had tended her wounds. Because she tried like crazy to beat him at gin, and enjoyed it so much when she did.

Because he'd lost interest in reason, logic and honor, and he was going to kiss her.

To give her time to react, to give himself one more sensation to remember, he cupped her cheek in his hand. He didn't close his eyes, so he knew that she did. He watched her lids drift down as her face tipped up. Watched her offer her mouth to him blindly.

Soft. He'd kissed a woman's mouth before, hadn't he? Yet no woman's mouth had ever felt so exquisitely soft before. He had to be careful with such a soft mouth. Court it. His tongue circled gently, testing, asking, and her lips parted under his. Slowly, easily, he slipped inside. And as simply as that, her taste caught him.

A bolt of feeling traveled up his spine and spread electrically through his limbs, making the hands that cupped her face tremble—a feeling like lust or lightning or fate. He plunged his tongue deeper, seeking more of her flavor, the secret, darker taste inside her mouth, an essence he hadn't known until this second that he'd needed all his life.

Mine. Her mouth, her taste—she was his—

She made a sound. Seth heard it, unsure if it meant joy or protest. He knew only her mouth, the feel of her face beneath his fingers, the hungry press of her body against his. Yes, she hurt, like he did. *Not here. The bed.* Without breaking contact with her mouth he dropped his hands from her face to circle her body and begin urging her that way.

A banshee howled outside.

Seth jerked erect. The sudden severance of the kiss left him scrambled, nerve endings twitching randomly, unable to sort the jumbled messages of mind and body. Sophie leaned against him. Her breath was as loud and hasty in his ears as his own. His sex jerked urgently.

That terrible, ululating howl came again. From the front porch.

Rocky?

"Stay here," he told Sophie, setting her away from him.

"Seth—"

"It's Rocky," he said tersely, starting for the door. "But something's wrong. She's never made a sound like that before."

What sounded like a chuckle—breathless, unsteady, but much like a chuckle—followed him. "She hasn't gone into labor around you before, I imagine."

Labor? Seth stopped short of the open doorway that framed a chunk of night, and said stupidly, "But I used up all the hot water when I washed the dishes."

Yes, that was a chuckle. Right behind him. "I don't think hot water is necessary with dogs, but—" she patted his arm as she passed him "—go ahead and boil some more if you want."

Rocky issued another of those ghastly howls.

"Oh, my God," Seth said.

Rocky was having her puppies, all right. All over the place.

Once the dog got her people outside, she stopped howling and began turning in circles. She had the first puppy while standing up on the porch. The process frightened her so much she took off down the steps and had the second one in the soft dirt nearby. The next two were born beside the storage shed. She managed to lie down for those, then she headed back to the porch, where she had the last one.

Since the dog obviously had no clue as to what she was supposed to do with those squirmy little bundles her body kept ejecting, Seth and Sophie had to collect the puppies and dry them. Fortunately, once the birthing itself was over, Rocky calmed enough under Sophie's soothing voice and hands to stay still while Seth brought the puppies to her. Either instinct or exhaustion took over. She let them nurse, and belatedly started licking them.

"You are one stupid dog," Seth said softly, kneeling on the weathered boards next to the blanket where Rocky was settled with her new family. The exhausted mother managed a couple of tired tail thumps in response.

Sophie didn't know who was more worn-out, her or the new mother. She'd moved around more in the last hour than she had in the past four days—or her entire life, if you counted a lifetime in memories. But the exhaustion wasn't unpleasant. She felt weighted and lethargic and successful. She and Seth had saved the puppies, and now it was good just to sit in the rocker and watch Seth petting his dog.

He was in profile to Sophie. The fuel in the lantern he'd brought outside was low, and its fitful glow sent shadows crawling over the side of his face she saw, the damaged side. Sophie recognized vaguely that some people might find him disturbing, even sinister. But his dark hair was drawn back and tied at the nape of his neck, and she was both fascinated and inexplicably comforted by the revealed lines of his face.

Purity. It was an odd word to apply to a man, but that was what she thought of when she studied his face. A purity of strength, of honor...the scars highlighted by the shifting play of light and shadow along his cheek and jaw didn't dispel her impression. They just made her sad.

So much pain. He'd been so dreadfully hurt...and was still hurting.

"I never saw an animal with such deficient instincts," he murmured, giving Rocky another rub behind the ears.

"She's probably too young," Sophie answered absently, her attention on the hand that stroked the dog. "Nature doesn't always get it right, you know. Some dogs go into heat as young as six months.''

"Well, nature sure missed the boat with this hound," he said, turning his head to look at Sophie, a slight smile on his lips.

When his eyes met hers, everything changed. Twin flames, reflections from the lamp, danced on the shiny darkness of his eyes. Her breath halted, then resumed at a different pitch as she inhaled heat along with air. Exhaustion fell away from her, and she ached with an awakening so huge it seemed her pores expanded in the effort to breathe him in.

She wanted him. Oh, how she did want him. And maybe...

He stood. Her gaze slipped down his body, and with a prescience like pain, she knew that body—knew the saltiness of his skin, and wanted to touch her mouth to him to remind herself of the precise taste. Knew the bunch and roll of his muscles as he moved, and wanted to remember their feel with her hands. With her body, beneath his. She lifted her eyes to his once more, and let him read on her face what she knew, what she wanted. What she hadn't yet dared to put into words for herself.

He went still. Her heart thundered in her chest as she looked up at him, offering. Then he spoke, his voice rough. "You'd better go to bed."

"I don't want to." She stood in the puddle of light cast by the lamp on the table beside her. "Not alone."

He didn't respond, not with words. She saw a muscle jump along his jaw. Saw his hands knot into fists at his sides, and the flare of heat in his eyes, and felt his tension almost as keenly as her own. "Come to bed with me," she whispered, wondering at herself, if this was courage or extreme folly.

"No."

That was all the answer he gave her—that one word—and the step that he took away from her, back into the shadows. She withstood his silence as long as she could, then turned and fled into the cabin, and the faulty privacy of his bed.

The sun was warm, the grass was brittle with autumn, the air was dry and cool, and Sophie was determined to be careful.

Maybe she'd been rash in her other life, she thought as she slowly shredded one long stalk of yellow-brown grass. She didn't know, but it seemed possible, judging by her behavior last night. She didn't have to stay that way. She could change, become more responsible. More deliberate.

Sophie sat on the porch steps in the warm, weak sun. Behind her, Rocky and the puppies slept. Seth's pickup was there, but he was gone. He must have left on some errand before she woke up, and that, surely, was smart of him. No doubt he was embarrassed by her behavior last night. She was, too, or at least she felt sure she would be once she saw him again.

Right now she felt peculiar. As if she had a gyroscope in her middle, spinning the way a gyroscope does, so fast it seems to stand still, and that spinning, humming center of her was slightly tilted.

As if she'd been tilted ever since Seth kissed her last night.

Behind her, the puppies yelped their tiny, mewling cries. She looked over her shoulder. Rocky had stood up, dislodging her clinging babies, and stared out across the little meadow, her tail wagging happily. Sophie followed the dog's gaze.

Seth stepped out from the small stand of pines. He carried a mesh bag filled with some sort of plant stuff, and wore a long, scabbarded knife at his belt. She supposed whatever was in the bag was his excuse for leaving the cabin this morning. As she watched him approach she forgot she expected to be embarrassed. Forgot the hurt that had followed her into sleep last night. Forgot everything in the simple pleasure of watching the sunlight sink into the blackness of his hair, watching the smooth cleverness of his muscles as they carried him over the rough ground.

The gyroscope in Sophie's middle lurched and spun faster. She stood and smiled. "Hello."

Seth felt Sophie's smile like a punch in the gut. It reminded him of the first smile he'd seen on her face, the first time she opened her eyes and saw him. He saw trust, and what looked very much like joy. And one thing more. Something that hadn't been there the first time—arousal.

How, he wondered desperately, was he going to keep from taking what he was so hungry for, when he knew that she, too, hungered? Still. In spite of last night. In spite of the bruised, sleepless look beneath her eyes that accused him, even if her smile did not.

"What's in the bag?" she asked.

"Seed pods." He managed to keep his face still. At least she didn't have to know how he responded to her. "Could you keep this crazy dog from tripping me while I put this in the drying shed?" Rocky was greeting Seth enthusiastically, pressing against his bad leg in a way likely to cause disaster.

"Oh." For one more heartbeat, her eyes searched his, then fell. "Sure. C'mere, Rocky."

His drying shed abutted the back of the cabin. He listened to Sophie talking to Rocky and the pups while he sorted through the utterly useless seed pods he'd brought back. He didn't have another garden or naturalization project planned. He had no use for the seeds he'd gathered. He'd just needed to get away.

When the sound of Sophie's voice stopped he felt an unreasonable lurch of panic. He hurried in the cabin's back door.

The front door stood open like usual, and now he could hear her voice again, a low, affectionate murmur addressed to Rocky. The tightness in his chest eased.

What had he thought? That she'd disappeared as mysteriously as she'd come into his life? Scowling, Seth went to the fire pit. An iron hook held the coffeepot over the remnants of the fire he'd kindled early that morning. He checked and found the pot half-full, which meant Sophie must have made a pot after he left. He poured two cups before going to the front door.

She sat on the smooth boards of the porch next to the proud new mother and her five squirming babies. Today she wore worn blue cotton and torn emerald silk—another of his work shirts, and the badly mended remains of her own silk pants.

She took his breath away. Seth paused in the doorway until he found his voice. "I'm pretty low on provisions. I'll go into town today." He handed her one of the mugs, then stood beside her and sipped from the other, watching her out of the corner of his eye. "Coffee's good." If you liked road tar. He forced himself to take another sip.

She didn't look at him. "You've got to be kidding."

He sighed. Restoring her comfort with him was not going to be easy. "Make a list of things for me to pick up in town today. Clothes, makeup, that sort of thing."

"Don't be silly." She set her mug down and stood. "There's no point in you getting me anything. I'm sure I'll be out of your hair, back in my old life, in another day or two."

No, this was definitely not going to be easy. "We need to talk about last night."

She went still. "About contacting the sheriff?"

"That, too."

Now she faced him, and it wasn't hurt that flashed in her green eyes. It was temper. "Is this where you apologize? Or maybe you're going to tell me you didn't want to take advantage of me."

Since that was pretty much what he'd had in mind, he kept quiet.

"Last night you said all that needed to be said in one word—*no*. Let's not get into postmortems now." Her eyes glistened with tears that her scowl warned him not to notice. "I don't make an offer like that every day, you know. Or I guess you don't—and you probably don't think I can know that, either, since I can't remember and I'm probably a d-damned drug dealer and—"

"Shh." He did the only thing that occurred to him—set his coffee on the porch rail and reached for her.

She pushed him away. "No," she said. "No, dammit, you can't touch me anymore. Not unless you mean it."

Oh, he meant it, all right. But he was trying his damnedest not to do what he was sure she'd regret. He said nothing.

She stared at him, her green eyes as unblinking as a cat's, for a long moment. "Don't go into town yet," she said abruptly.

"Why not?"

"Because once you do, I become part of the rest of the world again." She turned away. "I don't want to let the world in yet. Does that make any sense to you? Besides—" she glanced at him, her smile tentative "—I don't know what size I wear. Why not wait and see if I have another memory flash about shoe size or something?"

If he didn't get away from her, he was going to touch her. And mean it. "I'm out of groceries," he said. "And we can guess at your sizes. But I won't bring the world back with me. I won't talk to the sheriff about you."

She looked...disappointed. In him. She turned and went inside the cabin without speaking.

Five

They stumbled through the morning awkwardly. There were too many topics to avoid—like what hadn't happened last night, and Sophie's past, and Seth's reasons for isolating himself in this cabin. Avoiding those subjects took a lot of concentration and left them with long silences to ignore.

Right after lunch, while Seth was arguing with Sophie over whether she was well enough to do the dishes, the propane truck came. Seth went outside to talk with the driver, so Sophie won that argument by default.

She lost the next one. Seth flatly refused to let her go into town with him. "Unless," he said, "you've decided to go to the sheriff. But if you're going to stay here with me while we wait to hear from my cousin, you need to stay out of sight."

He was right, of course. She didn't really know why she'd tried to persuade him otherwise, when she didn't want him going into town at all—except she thought that if the world was going to break into their solitude, they should meet it together. When she saw his truck disappear around the cor-

ner of the mountain that afternoon, it felt like she was the
one growing smaller in the distance, not him. Smaller, more
helpless—and a great deal less safe.

She didn't like what that said about her dependence on
him.

When Seth pulled up in front of the cabin, shadows
stretched across the yard, lazy and elongated like waking
cats. He'd been gone longer than he'd planned, and he
hoped she hadn't worried.

He really should get a phone put in, he thought as he let
down the tailgate and reached for one of the boxes of groceries. Being late wouldn't be so bad if he'd been able to
call—

He stopped with the box half-out of the truck. He was
thinking about getting a phone so he could call Sophie when
he was going to be late? What kind of idiocy—oh, no, he
thought, grimacing as he heaved the full-packed box up into
his arms and started for the steps. No, he'd gone over this
ground thoroughly on the drive into town. He was not going to let her proximity and his own long-unmet needs get
him started expecting anything. He knew himself. He knew
he tended to see physical intimacy as more than it was.
Linda had been the proof of that, hadn't she?

No, for both Sophie's sake and his own he couldn't have
her, not in the expressly carnal way he wanted to have her.
Simple physical intimacy wouldn't be simple, and there was
no way he could have more. No way he deserved more.

Rocky thumped her tail at him as he mounted the porch,
but she didn't get up. Seth wondered why Sophie hadn't
come out. She must have heard the truck. Was she sulking?

The air smelled of smoke.

Not the pleasant blend of wood smoke, either—an acrid,
scorched smell. Fear jumped in his chest and grabbed him
by the throat. "Sophie?" He dropped the box he was carrying. *Smoke!* The past leapt into the present just as that
wall of flame had exploded two years ago. *Not again—he*

couldn't fail again. He plunged through the door that always stood open and looked around frantically.

"Hi," Sophie said in a small voice.

She sat in the rocker beside the empty fire pit. Nearby stood the old ironing board he dragged out when he absolutely had to. On the ironing board rested his iron and what looked like one of his shirts. On the floor was at least one more shirt, and on her cheeks were tear tracks.

"Sophie?"

"I'm sorry." She sniffed. "I'm an idiot. I tried—I just wanted to make things nice for when you got back, but I b-burned the goulash and I burned your shirt when I tried to iron it and then—then I burned *another* shirt, so you see I really am worse than helpless because I just—"

"Sophie." He went to her—he didn't notice doing it, but there he was in front of her, lifting her out of that chair, pulling her up against him, warm, so warm... "It doesn't matter. What does a shirt or two matter?"

Her head was pressed against his chest, at just the right spot for his hand to cup the back of it gently. "I can't cook," she said, her voice still wobbly with tears.

He smiled over her head at the cabin around them, and his heart squeezed. "You cleaned out the fire pit."

"Yes." She hesitated. "I saw you carry trash out the back door this morning, so I put the ashes in one of those big barrels out back."

"That's great." He usually put the wood ash in the compost pile rather than in his trash-burning barrels, which had to be hauled to the dump and emptied, but this didn't seem like the time to explain about trash disposal. His hand moved, irresistibly, up the back of her head in a lingering caress. "And you cleaned up in here, too, didn't you?"

"I mopped." Her voice took on a more hopeful note. "That part went okay, and so did the dusting. I figured out how to use your washing machine, and when I took the ashes out back I saw the clothesline. So I hung your shirts out to dry after they were clean. They smelled so good, Seth, like fresh air. Then I went and burned them.''

"It doesn't matter."

"But I wanted to do something for you."

She was doing something *to* him right now—and if she was too preoccupied to notice, it wouldn't be long before—

She lifted her head. "Seth?" Her eyes shone damply with questions. Then her arms went around him and she pulled herself tight against him, answering those questions herself.

His breath caught as a purely human fire raced through him, from his groin up his spine, down his legs and arms. "You shouldn't . . ." It was all he could do not to grab her bottom and grind himself against her. "Shouldn't have worked so hard, sweetheart. You're not really over being hurt yet."

"I'm fine." Her hands, sliding up his back to his shoulders, urging him to bend down, to explore the face she turned up to his, told him how fine.

Seth didn't hear any small voices at the back of his mind reminding him of what he'd so firmly decided earlier. He didn't feel any twinge of conscience or pity or self-preservation. All he knew was an aching imperative that turned his blood to fire and left him heavy and aching. All he saw was the hope on her face as his head lowered.

His Beauty wanted a kiss.

Sweet. Her hunger had a flavor he'd craved since his first taste of her. He courted that flavor, that heat, now—courted it with his tongue and his lips as his mouth mated with hers, with his hands that flowed down her back to her hips, pressing firmly into her soft flesh.

When he lifted his head her lips were damp and swollen. Her face glowed. She wanted this, wanted him, and he wanted her. Right or wrong, he wanted her. Seth ran his hand down her arm to her hand. He caught her fingers in his, lifted her hand and kissed the palm. Then he took her by the hand and led her to his bed.

Standing beside the bed, they kissed. Seth kept pulling his head back just so he could have the delirious pleasure of rejoining her mouth one more time. She went up on tiptoes, so he helped, one arm half-lifting her. The feel of her body against his was a luxury too profound to waste by rushing. She eased away from him and a moment's panic spurted through him, but then she lay down on his bed. He smiled to see her stretched out, waiting for him, one of her hands resting on the pillow next to her head, her silk-clad legs restless.

He started to unbutton his shirt, then froze, trying to remember.

"What is it?" She sat up. "Seth? What's wrong?"

"Just a minute." His shirt hung loose as he sat on the bed and pulled out the drawer in the bedside table. Hastily he dug through the contents. No sign of... "Ah." He set two of the foil-wrapped packets on the table. "I wasn't sure I still had these. It's... been awhile."

"Seth." From behind she wrapped her arms around him, leaning into him. The living weight of her excited him. So did the warmth of her breath on the back of his neck.

He turned quickly, capturing her mouth with his, and pressed her down into the bed. The feel of her beneath him, submitting to his strength and exerting her own with her busy hands, her hungry mouth and excited writhings, sent him half-over the edge. His hands shook as he pulled back enough to unfasten her shirt. His sense of luxurious leisure evaporated in the rising heat, but he still intended to go slowly. For her.

As he unfastened the third button, her hands slid up to his shoulders, then down, pulling his shirt with them. Then her hands slipped away, and she stilled.

He went rigid. His shoulder—she could see the scars. His eyes flew from the soft skin he had been uncovering to her face.

She smiled. The smile seemed to fill her, tipping up the corners of her mouth, weighting the corners of her eyes with languid arousal. The cream of her skin flushed with her smile. One of her hands lay next to her head, and the way the fingers curled inward made Seth think they were smiling, too, in the boneless, contented way a cat smiles with its entire body.

She was not repulsed, no. Instead she waited, lazy with heat, for him to undress her. Slowly his hands resumed their task, and now he watched her face instead of her body. When he pushed the shirt aside, her breath hitched, and he saw in her eyes how badly she wanted him to see her, to touch her. He looked down.

Beautiful. He'd seen her breasts before, but they were even more beautiful now, when he knew she bared them to him willingly. Then, he had very nearly kissed them. Now he would. He bent.

She sighed his name, her hands lifting to tangle in his hair. Then again... "Seth, I—"

"No." The kiss he pressed on her lips was gentle, but his muscles were tense. "No words, Sophie. Words can too easily sound like promises." He had no right to either—not the words or the promises.

Her hands were still in his hair. Gently, wordlessly, she urged his head to her breast.

He took her into his mouth.

Never, afterward, was Seth able to separate the jumble of moments that followed, sort them into sequential order. Arms and legs moved against and with each other, hers and his, sweat slick and urgent. There were sounds she made, sounds he made, the pungent smell of arousal, the feel of her slick heat on his hand as he pushed her higher, further. The feel of her nipple in his mouth, her hands in his hair, on his face. His hips. The burn of her hand on his arousal, and the different tastes of her that filled him—the underside of her breast, the pounding pulse at her throat, the scented skin of her inner thighs. All of that and more collided in unsorted moments, as if he had somehow slipped time's leash for the duration of his madness.

One moment stood clear, unique, shattering. One moment hinged his past with his future, and changed all the moments of his life that would come. One moment he was poised above her, probing the entrance to her mysteries, and the next—

The next he was inside, and she closed around him, perfectly tight and throbbing. He cried out—or she did—and then the currents seized his body and sent him, and her, out over their heads, where the undertow was terrible and glorious. He saw her face as she went under, felt her convulse, and then the whirlpool seized him, and he drowned with her.

Seth woke up late the next morning. He blinked, confused by the sunshine streaming through the window. He never slept in.

His hand swept out automatically across the rumpled sheets.

She wasn't there.

He sat up quickly, then heard her on the porch humming an off-key version of another country song. He exhaled slowly, wondering how long he'd panic when she was out of his sight. How long would it matter? She had another life. Sooner or later, she'd go back to it.

When he shoved away the covers and swung his feet off the bed, the movement sent a renewed whiff of sexual musk through the air. His mouth twisted in something like a smile, but it wasn't much like the smiles she'd given him last night.

This was the morning after. And if she didn't have regrets yet, she would. Eventually, when her memory came back.

With his propane tank full again, he could take a hot shower for the first time in days. But the abundance of hot water failed to soothe him. When he went to the kitchen, the sight of the cutting board covered with crumbs and a smear of strawberry jam made him even edgier. How had he slept so hard he didn't know when she left the bed? Didn't hear her making coffee or getting breakfast?

The air outside held the crisp benevolence of autumn. He carried two mugs of freshly brewed coffee out on the porch, where Sophie sat with Rocky and the pups again. She had on one of his shirts instead of the clothes he'd bought for her yesterday. "It's chilly out here," he told her. A breeze fluttered the tail of the shirt he wore, which he'd left unbuttoned. "I'll get you a jacket."

"I'm fine." Her smile looked as automatic and meaningless as her words sounded.

Was she fine? He crossed the porch to her. "You fixed yourself breakfast, I noticed."

"I sliced some bread and spread it with jam." She reached up to take the mug he handed her, but her eyes didn't lift to his. "I don't seem to be very culinary. I couldn't think of anything else to fix." She turned back to the puppies and stroked one with her finger. "Seth, I—I'm sorry."

Oh, God. He'd thought he was expecting this, was prepared for it. He'd been wrong. Without speaking, Seth turned and headed for the door.

"Seth?"

He stopped in the doorway without looking back. "You said you weren't interested in postmortems."

"That's not what I meant." She'd followed him. Her hand lit uncertainly on his arm. "I'm sorry, that's all. Sorry I threw myself at you and practically forced you to—with all my problems I had no right, no right at all involving you that way. You were just feeling sorry for me because of the way I was sniveling, and I—"

"Sophie." He turned and pulled her up against him. "Last night had nothing to do with pity. Can't you tell when a man's taking advantage of you?"

Her voice was muffled against his chest. "I guess not. Is that what you did?"

He bent his head to rest his cheek—his good one, the one on his right—against the fluff of her bright hair, and nodded. "Damn straight."

"Oh." Tension flowed from her body like syrup from a bottle. Her arms slipped around his waist, and she turned her head to rest her face against his chest. For a few minutes they stood and held each other and watched Rocky's babies in silence. Three of the puppies were nursing. The other two had fallen asleep with the teats still in their mouths. Soon the three joined the two, and Rocky gave a huge sigh and closed her eyes, as well.

Seth was almost content. The throb of desire built slowly, easily. He thought about taking her back inside, back to the big bed he'd just gotten out of. Then Sophie spoke. "My memories aren't really gone."

He lifted his head, shocked.

"I can't touch them," she said without moving. "But I feel them pressing in on me sometimes. This morning when I woke up...it felt like my skull was too small. Like the past was trying to squeeze in, to climb back in here with me. That's how it seems—as if I'm here, inside my head, and the memories are out there somewhere, trying to get back in. But I don't want them." Her fingers curled into his shirt, and she held on.

"Why not?" he asked softly.

She was silent so long he didn't think she'd answer. "Because everything will change when I remember. And I want a little more time."

He was tempted, so very tempted, to help her hide from herself just a little longer. It would be wrong. He knew that. But how much would one more day, or two, matter?

The distant bass rumble of thunder rolling in over the mountains brought his head up. He looked out at a line of dark clouds to the north, and felt the wind pick up. "It's going to storm again," he said, his arms tightening around her. He watched the tattered edges of clouds as the wind whipped the storm front closer. "The weatherman claimed the front would miss us, but it's headed this way fast." A fierce exultation rose in him to match the rising wind.

She met his eyes. "Is that unusual for around here? Two storms so close together?"

"Yes," he said. *I'll let her go when the time comes,* he promised himself.

"Are we going to be cut off from everything again?"

"Oh, yes." But thank God that time wasn't yet. Not yet.

She smiled.

He bent and caught that smile with his mouth.

Two hours later they were outside, in his experimental grove on the west side of the cabin. A protective hedge of prickly algerita, Seth's second line of defense against hungry critters, fenced three dozen silvery barked Mexican persimmons. The dark clouds he'd spotted earlier were rolling in, and he was trying to finish harvesting seeds for next spring's planting.

Sophie worked one row over from him. She hummed a Garth Brooks song off-key, and her pants kept trying to fall down. She stuffed some fruit in the mesh bag that hung from her shoulder. When she straightened with a handful of the tiny red persimmons, she had to tug her jeans up with the other hand.

Seth bent his head, hiding a smile. She was anything but a fashion plate in the clothes he'd gotten her yesterday. He'd automatically bought Linda's size, which was definitely not Sophie's.

Fortunately he'd known better than to tell Sophie that.

He watched her now as she carried the handful of bright fruit to her mouth and nibbled. "You're eating my research," he observed mildly.

She froze. "These are from one of the other bushes, not the one you told me to pick from. You didn't need them, did you?" she asked anxiously. "You said you only kept the seeds from the bushes with the largest fruit."

"Trees, Sophie. Not bushes. Even if they don't look like it. This year I had three trees that were keepers—this one, the one you're picking from, and its next-door neighbor. The one that produced the fruit you just swallowed.''

She stared at her hand, so stricken he almost laughed. ''Don't worry about it. I'd already harvested that one. The few persimmons still on it don't matter.''

''Then why—?'' She narrowed her eyes at him and grabbed two berry-sized fruits from her small handful and threw them at him.

They both missed. He did laugh then.

She grinned as smugly as if she'd hit her target and wandered over, nibbling on her stolen fruit. ''These are delicious.''

''They're a lot sweeter than regular persimmons,'' he agreed. ''That's why I'm trying to breed a cultivar that bears larger fruit. Are you finished with that tree, or just goofing off?''

''I'm finished. Why do you call this just a hobby, Seth?''

''I can't very well earn a living with it,'' he said tersely.

''Do you need to?'' she asked, tilting her head to one side.

What he needed was something to do with his life. Something that mattered. He liked working with native plants, seeing what he and nature together could come up with. It just wasn't enough. ''Most of us weren't born rich.'' He stood. ''If you're finished—''

''No, I'm not! Why are you so blasted evasive? Why don't you just tell me what you do for a living?''

Two years of silence gripped him. He had no idea he intended to break it. ''Nothing. I don't do a damned thing now. I used to be a fire fighter.''

She stepped closer. ''That's where you got your paramedic training?''

He didn't answer, appalled with himself. Next she'd ask about—

''Is that how you were hurt?'' Her eyes softened. She lifted a hand toward his face.

He jerked back. ''The rain's nearly here. Let's get these to the drying shed.''

* * *

That night Sophie lay in Seth's arms, listening to the song of the wind in the trees. The cabin was utterly dark except for the reddish glow from the banked coals in the fireplace. Seth slept. His big body heated her all along her back, but her face felt the nip from the air let in by the open front door.

He said he left it like that for Rocky's sake. Sophie knew better. Seth needed that door open for himself. She didn't know if his need came from whatever accident had scarred him, or if the open door had some other, more subtly powerful meaning for him.

She didn't know *yet*. But she would.

Outside, the night was complete, as it is in only a few places that are far from city lights and lack atmospheric haze, either natural or man-made. Inside, Sophie was helping Seth fix supper. They'd been lovers for two days.

Surely she'd never been this happy. Sophie didn't need memories to know that the past two days were gifts—rare and precious gifts. Seth was opening up to her. Trusting her. He'd been a fireman, he'd said. He hadn't told her how he got hurt, but she was sure—

"Ow." She lifted her finger to her mouth.

"What?" Seth set down the knife he was boning the chicken with. "Did you hurt yourself?"

"Of course not." It had hardly bled at all. She picked up the potato peeler again. "I'm getting pretty good with the vegetables. You'll have to teach me how to do the meat next."

He raised both eyebrows. "You want me to let you use a knife?" He spoke with such dry disbelief that she laughed, and he smiled back.

Seth smiled sometimes now. He'd even laughed twice. The sight of his smile gave the gyroscope in her middle a fresh spin. "You'd better watch out," she said, "smiling at me that way. That's incitement, Seth Brogan." Then she could have kicked herself, because the smile faded on one side. The damaged side.

The fool man still didn't believe what the sight of him did to her, how much she wanted him. She'd have to show him. "I warned you." She slapped the peeler down on the chopping block next to the unevenly peeled potato and started toward him. "Don't say I didn't warn you."

"What are you doing?"

"Attacking you." She stopped about three heartbeats away from him, close enough to feel his body heating the air between them. The itchy music of desire hummed under her skin. She lifted her hands to the buttons of his shirt. "I've wanted to seduce you all day, but you make that very difficult, Seth."

"I do?" He watched her hands bemusedly. "For God's sake, tell me what I'm doing wrong. I'll stop."

She reached the bottom of his shirt and tugged to free it from his jeans. "You're too willing. It isn't seduction when the victim is willing." She shoved his shirt off.

He was so perfect, inside and out. His body was magnificent, of course. He was also bossy, moody, full of secrets... fierce, gentle, passionate.

Perfect. She ran her hands up his arms, and the strength there excited her. His shoulders invited her exploration, too, but she didn't miss his slight stiffening when she caressed scarred skin along with smooth. "Good muscle definition here," she told him with a nod, running her hands down his chest. Desire tightened another notch, edging into hunger. She wanted him so badly. Again. Already. She raised her eyes to let him see.

He reached for her.

"No." She pushed his hands down. "I explained about seduction. Be still."

"I don't know if I can." If humor edged his voice, something much rougher underlay it.

"Try." She bent and licked his nipple.

He went rigid. She felt his muscles tighten hard with need as she splayed her hands on his chest and knew a rush of hunger, felt the hasty beat of his heart and knew the mad acceleration of her own. Sweet exhilaration sped through her. Taking charge like this was like being both the pinwheel and the wind—she was dizzy, powerful, reckless with speed.

She sent her hands racing over him. Her mouth. "I want you," she said, pausing to lap at his other nipple. "I ache."

All of a sudden she wasn't on her feet anymore. The world did a quick spin and she was in his arms. He strode quickly for the bed.

"Hey!" She tugged at his hair. "What happened to my seduction?"

"You're right. I'm not any good at being seduced." He dropped her onto the bed and followed her down so fast she lost her breath.

Or maybe it was the look in his eyes that took her breath away. "I'll have to practice," he growled, unsnapping her jeans and pulling them down. "Later."

He was climbing the ladder again.

Martinez and Grisham heeled it in at the bottom. Sweat ran down his back and forehead, detoured from his eyes by his face mask. He sucked in hot, metallic air from the tank on his back as he climbed—slowly. He tried to hurry, but his feet advanced at the same measured pace, in spite of the voice at the back of his brain that told him to hurry, hurry.

At first he could barely hear that voice over the noise the monster was making. The fire's bass roar mixed with the battering hiss of one hundred gallons of water per minute hitting wood the monster had heated to nearly thirteen hundred degrees Fahrenheit.

As he reached the top of the ladder the voice got louder, more frantic. He tried to hurry. He tried.

His got his legs locked on the rungs properly, leaving his arms free. Hobbs was behind him on the ladder because there were two victims in the second-story bedroom, and the fire roared its lust for destruction on the floor beneath. They were damn near out of time.

All familiar. Like the horror gnawing at his brain, the desperate voice inside that knew, that remembered, but could never stop the sequence once it had begun.

Smoke poured out the window. That's all he saw at first, the swirling clouds of smoke, though the distant shriek at the back of his mind knew that wasn't how it had happened the first time. But that's how it happened all the other times he came here.

He leaned forward, into the window. Slowly, agonizingly slowly. It was like pushing against time, against an invisible wall of fate and inevitability. Then he saw the faces.

Two girls. One, barely into her teens, with terrified eyes and dark hair. One younger, very young, in a white and pink nightgown. The older girl held the little one.

Seth pushed harder, harder. Like the popping of a bubble, the resistance gave way. He reached both arms out.

The littlest girl screamed. She tried desperately to get away, and the older girl could barely hang on to her— couldn't pass her to Seth because the little one squirmed away too frantically.

No time. No time. The words beat in his ears like a pulse. He shoved his face mask off and breathed in poisonous heat. "There, sweetheart," he crooned. "I'm just a man under all this stuff. Not a beast or a monster. Come on, sweetheart, let me get you out of here."

He felt her slight weight in his arms. Then the hell-wall exploded.

Seth had been up for hours when he heard Sophie moving around inside. He was out on the porch, smoothing a pine board that would become part of a tabletop, when her off-key humming reached him, followed by sounds from the kitchen part of the cabin. He paused to listen, the plane hovering above the wood clamped in his vise, then went back to his task.

The dream didn't come very often anymore. He thought he handled it well enough when it did show up. Keeping busy helped. He'd never been able to stop thinking about it entirely, but he didn't let himself dwell on the dream.

He'd finished that board and was clamping the next one in place when she came out, carrying two coffee cups. She wore one of his shirts and a smile.

He hoped there had been some coffee left from the pot he'd made earlier. Sophie's culinary skills so far extended to peeling, cleaning and cutting up vegetables. Coffee making was an art still beyond her.

"Hi there, sailor," she said in an intentionally sultry voice, holding out one of the cups. "Remember me?"

He couldn't smile back. When she handed him the mug, her fingers brushed his. The touch made him vaguely nauseous. Not because of her. Because of him. He looked away.

"Seth?" Her voice was her own again. "What's wrong?"

"Nothing," he said, and the lie tasted as foul as he felt. He looked out over the fall of rocks to the west. The path that climbed past those boulders was the one he'd taken the night he went looking for his damn fool dog—and found Sophie. "I need some time to myself," he said at last. "I'm not used to... so much company."

"Company? Is that what I am?"

He made himself look at her. "Sophie," he started, without knowing how he would finish, what he could say. Rocky's low growl stopped his groping for words he didn't have. He turned to see what was bothering her.

The dog's head and hackles were raised. A low growl rumbled in her chest as she stared down the rutted road. "Someone's coming." Seth felt the alarm deep inside, in a place he didn't remember ever touching before. Because the fear was for Sophie, he was able to put aside the poisonous remnants of the dream. He started toward the steps. "Go inside."

"But—"

"Now, Sophie." He turned his head to meet her eyes, willing her to hurry. "No one knows you're here. Best if we keep it that way."

Her face expressionless, she nodded and vanished into the cabin.

Together, man and dog watched the point where the dirt road disappeared around a corner of mountain about seventy feet from the porch.

The noise of the motor preceded the Jeep. Then a rugged army-style vehicle with battered paint, a roll bar instead of a roof, and a driver wearing a black Stetson bounced into view along the rutted curve. Seth waited as it approached the cabin and pulled to a stop directly in front.

The man who got out of the Jeep was taller than Seth and leaner. That, and the way he moved, made him look like a half-starved dog—or a grizzled wolf. The brim of his hat shadowed his face so that all that showed was a bristly mustache peppered with gray above a stern mouth. "You don't have much road left in a couple places," he told Seth. "Just mud."

The sight of him changed the nature of Seth's alarm without diminishing it. "Tom," he said to his cousin, starting down the steps. "I didn't expect to see you anytime soon."

"Raz told me you called," the man said, joining Seth in front of the steps. "And why. If your mystery guest is still here, I need to see her." His head turned, angling up just enough that the sunlight now struck beneath the hat's brim, revealing a craggy face that suited the rangy body.

He was looking over Seth's shoulder. Seth turned and saw Sophie standing in the doorway, one hand clutching his shirt at the neck, holding it together in the slight breeze while she leaned against the doorway for support, her face pinched and pallid.

Seth's cousin spoke. "Miss Cochran." His voice was rough and cool and polite. "I was sorry to hear you'd been injured, ma'am. I'm afraid I need to take you back to Houston for questioning."

Six

Pain. Pressure. Memory tightened down like a vise, squeezing until she was gasping for breath. Sophie held on to the door with what strength she could find, staring at the tall man with the old eyes...and she knew him, knew...

The pressure imploded with all the delicate finality of a soap bubble popping. Vaguely Sophie heard Seth's curses as he came to her. "Officer Rasmussin," she said to the other man, naming him as she was now able to name herself once more. She managed to straighten just as Seth reached her, and in straightening, she pulled away from him. Dizziness lapped at the edges of the world.

Officer Rasmussin was...the Houston Police Department detective she'd talked to after her sister's death, the man who— "You're Seth's cousin," she observed distinctly. Then she stepped forward, right into the swirling darkness.

* * *

She didn't like fainting. Not that she'd ever done it before, but, considering the way she felt as she came around, it wasn't a habit she meant to take up.

"...way to spring it on her," Seth growled.

She was on the couch. Seth sat beside her. She knew that without opening her eyes, because she felt the nubby weave of the upholstery beneath her, and she felt Seth's weight and heat on her left.

"How was I to know she'd pass out?" Detective Rasmussin said. "She must have known someone would come for her. She ought to be damned glad she isn't under arrest."

"Dammit, Tom, Raz must have told you about her memory being gone."

"He told me a lot of things. He didn't mention that you were involved with her. Or have I misunderstood why she's wearing your shirt and not a damn thing more?"

She fought the nausea that had bile rising in her throat, wanting, needing to hear Seth's reaction. But he didn't speak before the other man went on. "She knew who I was when she saw me. Right away. Face it, Seth, she's a damned good little actress. Not perfect, though." His voice altered its pitch. "You may as well open your eyes, Miss Cochran. I know you're awake."

"I'm keeping my eyes closed," she said clearly, "because I don't want to throw up."

"Get her some soda from the pantry," Seth told his cousin. "It's not cold, but it might help."

She heard the footsteps as the police detective left.

"Seth..."

"Shh." He brushed her cheek with his fingertips. "Take it easy. You've had a shock."

She made herself open her eyes. Her stomach roiled, but that wasn't the worst of it. The worst was seeing the look on Seth's face, all tight and closed. "I'm sorry," she whispered. "When I saw him—your cousin—everything hit me at once."

He hesitated. "Yes."

But she'd heard his hesitation as clearly as his agreement. And she didn't blame him, she didn't blame him at all for having doubts. She struggled to sit up.

Seth's hand was at her back immediately, helping her. She grimaced, fighting the upheaval in her stomach.

"Take it easy, Sophie. You don't have to—"

"Yes, I do. You deserve some answers." The nausea ebbed slightly. "Everything was trying to come back anyway. Seeing your cousin again just hurried it up. The last time I saw him, in Houston, I guess I'd already talked to half the Houston Police Department about my sister's death. Finally I was referred to him. He wasn't in charge of investigating her case specifically, but he's in some sort of special department—"

"The Special Investigations Squad," Tom Rasmussin said as he approached. He held out a glass. "Drink this."

The double whammy of sugar and caffeine did seem to help. When Tom took out his notebook she felt almost steady. Or maybe it was Seth's continued presence beside her that steadied her, though she hoped not. She couldn't lean on Seth anymore. "Are you going to read me my rights?"

"No, ma'am. You're not under arrest. Just wanted for questioning."

"Questioning about what?" She thought of a bag of white powder in Seth's cupboard and licked her dry lips. "Do I have to go back to Houston with you? Can't you ask your questions here?"

Seth's cousin watched her out of those pale, emotionless eyes that had so unnerved her after Christine's death. That was long before she knew Seth existed...Seth. She felt dizzy with memory, with two sets of memories. Seth loomed like a mountain range in her mind, dividing her life in two.

"I think you'll probably have to come in with me, Miss Cochran, but maybe not. Maybe you can clear everything up right now, since your memory has come back."

Only a trace of skepticism colored his words. It was enough. She knew he didn't believe anything had ever been wrong with her memory.

"Six nights ago," he said, "from what I was told, Seth found you on this mountain. Around midnight."

She nodded.

"We have several witnesses who place you with Charles Farquhar earlier that night. The next morning at ten o'clock, a park ranger found Farquhar's body several miles south of here, in Big Bend. He'd been shot—murdered."

His body? Charles was dead?

"In addition, your car turned up three blocks from Farquhar's apartment. So I do have several questions for you to answer, Miss Cochran."

She closed her eyes. She hadn't wished Charles dead, had she? No, she'd pursued him, but with the intention of bringing him to a legal form of justice, only...

She shuddered. It was a moment before she realized she was hanging on to Seth's hand. She didn't even try to make herself turn loose. "I'm Frances Sophia Cochran," she said, opening her eyes, "though I've never gone by my first name. I *remember*... so many things... my middle name was my mother's choice. She never would admit that she named me for a movie star. People with her background don't do that sort of thing, you know. I grew up in Houston with a dog, a sister, two loving parents, and a ton of money I wasn't really aware of—sort of "Leave It to Beaver" after Ward won the lottery. I was... incredibly naive for this day and age."

She paused to smile at the bittersweet tug of memory. "I remember all of that now. I remember you, and how and why my sister died—and why you wouldn't help me when I tried to get evidence against the man responsible for her death."

"You wanted us to set up a sting operation aimed at Charles Farquhar, and you wanted to be the bait."

"Yes." Blond, magnificent Charles, whose family wasn't as rich as it used to be. Charles, who had seduced Sophie years before he took up with her sister, before he'd added drugs to his other tools for using the young and the innocent. Charles, who had given Christine the drug that killed her. Just as he had destroyed other young girls.

Tom Rasmussin was talking. "Like I told you then, we can't use civilians that way. But you didn't let my refusal stop you, did you? You started seeing Farquhar again. What happened six nights ago? How did you wind up on Old Baldy?"

She knew, even as she spoke, that he wouldn't believe her. "Like I said, I remember my name, my background, everything... except what happened to me that night."

Tom's professional expression vanished. "Oh, come on, Miss Cochran, you're not starring in some damned soap opera, and I'm not—"

Seth's deep voice interrupted. "That's enough, Tom."

Tom turned his scowl on his cousin. "If you can't stay out of an official interrogation, I'll have to ask you to leave the room."

Seth's smile wasn't pleasant. "It's my room. And you're a few hundred miles outside your proper jurisdiction."

Two pairs of eyes met in challenge, one as colorless and unfathomable as winter, the other dark and compelling as midnight. "I can make this official," Tom said at last, "if I have to. For the lady's protection, if nothing else."

Sophie's shoulders tensed. "For heaven's sakes, 'the lady' is right here and perfectly able to speak for myself."

Tom's pale gaze swung back to her. "Fair enough. You have any objection to answering some questions, Miss Cochran? Or to returning to Houston?"

"No." There was no point in pretending she could hide any longer.

"Then tell me when this erratic memory of yours begins."

She looked down at her hands, clasped tightly in her lap. She remembered what she'd said to Seth about not knowing if she'd bitten her nails, or whether she'd ever worn an engagement ring.

Her mouth twisted unhappily. Charles hadn't offered her a ring. He hadn't had to. "You're right. I didn't let your refusal to help stop me. I knew Charles Farquhar was responsible for Christine's death—morally, if not legally. I knew she wouldn't be his last victim, either. So I read up about evidence and procedures. I intended to get proof that he was selling drugs." She shook her head, distantly marveling. "He was amazingly easy to fool. He actually believed I was interested in him again."

"It had been several years since the two of you were together, hadn't it? Not since soon after you graduated from college. Then you heard he'd begun dating your sister."

Was she imagining Tom Rasmussin's hostility? "Yes." Sophie had talked to some of her old crowd, people she hadn't associated with since her disastrous relationship with Charles ended. The things she'd learned about him had made her blood run cold...too late. She'd learned the facts about Farquhar too late.

Tom said it for her. "After dating Farquhar for about three months, Christine Cochran died when her heart burst after taking cocaine."

She didn't answer. Her jaw clenched, and so did her hand, around Seth's. She gripped it tightly.

"You said Farquhar preferred very young women, like your sister at the time of her death. She was eighteen, wasn't she?" Tom thumbed through his notebook. "I have your exact words. 'Charles isn't interested in women. He likes girls—above the age of consent, preferably, but always innocent. He likes to destroy innocence.' So it is surprising that he wanted to take up with you again. You're a little beyond being described that way."

"Dammit, Tom—" Seth burst out.

She slid her hand up Seth's arm, urging a restraint that, she could see by his clenched jaw, he didn't like. "Well past innocence, yes," she said. "But Charles has—or had—a huge ego. He didn't want me—thank God—but he liked the idea that I was desperate enough to hang around and accept whatever tidbits of his attention he tossed my way."

"And what kind of 'tidbit' did he toss you on the night he died?"

Rain, slashing her exposed skin. Branches. Headlights. A man's voice. A slick road, and blood on her face. The impressions were jumbled, and her head started to hurt for the first time in two days as she tried to force her way through them. "I—we were at a party. At Cissy's—that's Cissy Thompson, Mrs. Justin Thompson. Charles took a phone call. He said he had to leave early." She lifted a hand to her temple, trying to soothe the pain. "I thought it might be his supplier. I wanted to go with him."

"And did you?"

"I don't know." For the first time since she woke the morning after the storm and saw Seth's damaged face, the lack of memory stirred a flutter of panic. This time she felt truncated. Bereft.

And Tom Rasmussin looked as skeptical as ever.

"I'm telling the truth!" Her voice sounded faintly shrill. She swallowed. "I can't remember anything after he told me he had to leave the party early."

Tom closed his notebook. His eyes, when they met hers, told her she hadn't imagined his hostility. "See if you can't jog your memory between here and Houston, Ms. Cochran. If you didn't kill Farquhar, then someone else did. If it was someone else, it's probably the same person who injured you that night, which places you at the murder scene. And a murderer is apt to prefer the security of a bullet to relying on your amnesia story." He stood. "Do you have anything here you'll need to take with you?"

"At least one thing," Seth said quietly. "Me."

* * *

Rocky didn't object to having her pups moved to the bed of Seth's pickup. In fact, as soon as Seth put an old pillow and blanket in back, the dog jumped in, curled herself around three times, then lay down and looked at her people expectantly.

"There, girl," Sophia crooned as she settled the last of the puppies against its mother. "You knew we'd bring them to you, didn't you?"

"Maybe," Seth said dryly. "Or maybe she expected you to puppy-sit while I took her for a ride. That's the look she gets on her face when we go into town."

The feelings lumped up in her throat wouldn't let her look at him. She frowned as she knelt on the tailgate.

"Rocky will be fine," Seth said, misreading her expression. "She likes riding in the truck. Don't worry so much." His hands circled her waist. He lifted, and she was on the ground.

Because she wanted so much to stand there, close to him, she stepped back.

Their eyes met, and she knew he'd noticed. Neither of them spoke as he helped her into the cab of the truck. He closed the door, then his cousin called out something. Seth went over to the Jeep.

Sophia watched the two men talking beside the battered Jeep. She'd never have taken them for cousins. They didn't look alike, not in build or features, though there was a certain similarity of expression or the lack of it.

Were they talking about her?

She had a pretty good idea of what Tom Rasmussin might tell his cousin about her: a poor little rich girl with too much time on her hands, and no better sense than to believe the first charming man who promised to love her no matter what. A girl who got in over her head very quickly... how much did Rasmussin know about the year she'd spent under Charles Farquhar's spell?

He knew how she'd reacted to Christine's death. She'd gone a little crazy when she lost the last of her family. But not crazy enough to murder. Sophia shivered. Not that.

She watched Tom Rasmussin settle his hat on his head. Seth turned and started for the pickup where she waited. She didn't remember Rasmussin being this, well, this antagonistic before. He'd been businesslike when she met him a couple times after Christine's death, even sympathetic. But back then, she'd been the victim's grieving sister. Now she was a murder suspect at worst, an obstructive witness at best.

Seth got into the truck, closing the door with a solid, final-sounding thunk. "We'll go first, and Tom will follow."

She nodded, and they started. They'd reached the edge of the small meadow that was Seth's front yard when she spoke, breathless. "Stop a minute. Please."

He did, looking at her questioningly. She twisted around in the seat, staring back at the cabin. She'd never seen his home from this angle. It looked rugged and welcoming, nestled in its little valley. Chances were she'd never see it again.

Her eyes burned with goodbye as she faced forward, pulling the seat belt across and clicking it in place.

The road to the highway was muddy, impassable for anything but a four-wheel-drive vehicle. Neither of them spoke. At the highway they turned left, and Seth pushed a tape into the built-in stereo.

A cowboy sang in a clear baritone about facing the barren waste without a drink of water. She glanced at Seth. Country music, or even rock, wouldn't have surprised her, but she hadn't expected him to choose the mellow lament of old cowboy songs.

"We'll head up to I-10," he said. "Houston is better than twelve hours straight driving time from here, so with our late start we'll have to stay the night somewhere. Tom and I were arguing over whether to head for Austin or stay on I-10 on into San Antonio. Austin's a straighter route, but it's two-lane part of the way. You have a preference?''

''Damn,'' she muttered. Then, louder: ''Damn! If that isn't just like a man! Worrying about routes, and what's fastest, and—and totally ignoring . . . don't you want to ask me anything? How can you just take off like this without asking, without knowing something about—''

''Sophie.''

''You don't really know anything about me. I don't see how you can just take off like this.'' *Or how I can let you when I have no right, no right at all.* Her hands twisted in her lap.

''Well, we know for sure now that you're not forty.'' His sideways glance invited her to share the joke.

''Did you ask your cousin that?''

''He volunteered a few things while you were getting ready. I told him to keep it to himself for now. Seemed like I ought to hear your story from you.''

She almost cried. He was so good. ''I'm not even 'Sophie.' ''

'' 'Sophia' is almost the same.''

It wasn't, but how could she explain that? How could she make him see the difference between the happy girl whose father had called her 'Sophie' and the useless young woman she'd grown into? ''My father gave me the locket. No one has called me 'Sophie' since he died.''

''How long ago was that?''

''Six years. He and my mother were killed when their small plane crashed during my senior year in college.''

''It was just you and your sister after that?''

Christine. The ache of pain and guilt robbed her of speech. She nodded. For a while all she heard was the hush of the tires on the highway, and the sad sound of a cowboy pining for his lost love on the stereo. ''My parents were both only children. I have some distant cousins on my mother's side up north, but I don't know them.''

"I was ten when my folks died," Seth told her. "But I was lucky. I had an aunt and uncle who took me in."

"Did your cousins mind having to share their home and their parents all of a sudden?"

"Raz may have, a little. He's only a couple of years older than me, so there was some competition between us. Tom's older than Raz or me, which made a difference. I think Tom liked having me around because I was one more person to be in charge of. Tom likes being in charge."

"I doubt he succeeded." She smiled for the first time since Tom Rasmussin showed up. "You've really messed up my theories about the oldest child being the tyrant of the family, you know."

"Have I?" He paused. "I take it your sister was younger than you. Did she think you bossed her around?"

"Oh, yes." Sophia heard the brittleness in her voice, felt it in her bones. "My parents named me as her guardian. A colossal mistake on their part."

"How did she die?"

"From using cocaine. Weren't you paying attention when your cousin questioned me?"

"I listened, but what I heard didn't tell me why you feel responsible, Sophie."

"Sophia," she corrected him. " 'Sophie' is gone."

"Is she?" The tape clicked, paused, and then resumed playing on the other side. "So your sister was involved with this Farquhar."

She didn't answer. She wanted to go back to yesterday, to this morning before the memories crashed in and wrecked the happiest time she'd had since "Sophie" died, and an overprotected young woman named Sophia made a series of bad decisions. "Why didn't you show your cousin the cocaine you found on me?" she asked abruptly.

"Is that what's in that bag, then, Sophie? Cocaine?"

"You know it must be!" Everything exploded in her then—grief, anxiety, the painful, hopeless feeling for Seth she wouldn't name. "And I'm *Sophia,* damn you! Sophia. I want you to stop calling me Sophie!"

On the stereo that cowboy started singing about the West Texas town of El Paso. By the time Seth spoke she was half ashamed of her outburst. "No," he said quietly, and that was all he said. Very much as he had two nights ago.

By six-thirty that evening, when Seth pulled into the parking lot of the Holiday Inn at the outskirts of San Antonio, he and Sophie weren't speaking. Or at least she wasn't talking, and Seth, too long immersed in his own silence, didn't know how to break into someone else's.

He got out of the truck just as Tom pulled in behind them. Sophie apparently wasn't as eager as he was to stretch his legs, since she stayed put.

Not *Sophie,* according to her. Sophia. But Seth didn't see any "Sophia" when he looked at the woman who'd ridden next to him into San Antonio. He saw Sophie, guileless and hurting, self-convicted of some nameless crime.

Of course, if wealth was a crime she was guilty. They'd guessed right about her being from Houston's wealthy set. She was also in one hell of a lot of trouble. Which was why, he figured, they weren't speaking. She was determined to spare him the burden of her presence. He was determined to show her how wrong she was.

The sun hung low. Seth's shadow dragged long and attenuated behind him as he walked slowly to the lobby doors, enjoying the slightly achy stretch of muscles that had stiffened over the long drive. He waited for Tom.

"I can't believe you never get a ticket," his cousin said. "Makes me damned uncomfortable, violating the law the way I have to in order to keep up with you."

"Yeah, sure." Seth opened the door. A blast of air-conditioned air hit him in the face. "You're mad because I insisted on traveling in front, and you couldn't go at your usual bat-out-of-hell speed."

"If you're going to get us checked in," Tom said, stopping, "I think I'll walk around for a few minutes, get the kinks out."

Seth paused in the doorway to look where his cousin was looking. Sophie was climbing out of the pickup. The too-big jeans and shirt he'd bought her made her look like a little girl playing dress-up. "She's not going to run," he said.

"Maybe. And maybe you're thinking with your—"

"Shut up, Tom." They both watched Sophie go to the rear of the truck and climb over the tailgate. Rocky left her puppies and dog met woman in the bed of the truck, one wagging her tail, the other laughing, the pair of them as excited to be reunited as if they hadn't seen each other every couple of hours on the way here.

"If you were thinking straight, you'd know one of us had better keep an eye on her. If she isn't a killer, she's a target."

"I know," Seth said levelly. "That's why I didn't argue about her returning to Houston."

"She wouldn't be in as much danger if she could get a grip on that slippery memory of hers."

"Her story sounds peculiar, but—"

"Peculiar?" Tom shook his head. "More like convenient."

"Not too convenient if she's innocent."

Tom's mouth twisted as if he'd bitten into something sour. "I know she *looks* innocent, but dammit, Seth, you can't be dumb enough to go by how she looks. Don't you see just a bit of similarity between Sophia Cochran and Linda Haviston? Two rich, bored socialites willing to use or be used—"

"Her name," Seth said, "is Sophie."

"Not to the three hundred or so Houstonians who move in her circle, it isn't."

"It is to me."

Frustration, and the concern he wouldn't show any other way, pulled Tom's mouth into a straight line. "Oh, hell," he said at last, pulling his hat off and slapping it against his leg. "You were always mule stubborn, weren't you? Stay here and keep an eye on my witness, then, while I get our rooms."

Seth glanced into the lobby. The young woman behind the check-in desk kept tossing little glances his way. Once he would have found that flattering. Now he knew it for the sort of appalled fascination people exhibit when they slow down to drive past a highway accident. "I'll get the rooms."

Tom's gaze followed Seth's. He didn't comment on the clerk's covert attention. "Get two rooms—one for your *Sophie,* and an adjoining one for the two of us."

The corner of Seth's mouth tugged up. "You trying to chaperon us, Tom?"

"Damn straight," Tom muttered, and stalked back toward the Jeep and pickup.

Seth watched his cousin walk away. Tom would be even more suspicious if he knew about the bag of white powder his witness-suspect had been carrying when Seth found her, the powder that Seth had, in effect, lied about by omission. Seth felt that omission in his gut, a tearing of loyalties. He didn't think he'd ever lied to Tom before. Even as a teenager he'd leveled with the cousin who took a big brother's interest in his misdeeds—and on a couple of occasions had explained the facts about Seth's misbehavior with one hell of an uppercut.

Seth knew why he hadn't told Tom about the powder. For the same reason he was returning to Houston, a city he'd promised himself he would never set foot in again. Sophie was in danger. He had to protect her. He couldn't let her be hurt, couldn't risk her going to jail when he knew she wasn't a user or seller of drugs.

He couldn't let her go, period.

Seth stepped from the humid heat outside, letting the door close behind him. The unwelcome trappings of civilization surrounded him along with the artificially cool air of the motel's lobby.

His Beauty had made a big mistake. She'd given herself to the Beast, and he wasn't about to let her take her gift back.

Sophie sat in the sun-warmed bed of the pickup, petting an insistent Rocky. San Antonio's air was muggy and thick, hanging on to the day's heat even this late in the year. So different, she thought, from the crisp air of the mountains she'd just left behind.

So similar to the tenacious humidity she'd lived in most of her life.

Some small noise made her look up. Tom Rasmussin walked toward the truck, his black Stetson in one hand. The angle of the setting sun flooded the air with a ruddy orange. With that mellow color bathing his face, and without his hat hiding his features, the man looked almost approachable as he stopped next to the truck and leaned against the side of it.

Almost. Sophie eyed him warily. "Rocky doesn't seem to mind traveling. I was worried about bringing her and the puppies along, but she's doing great." They'd stopped several times to let the dog out along the side of the road, and each time Sophie had felt Seth's tension, as if he weren't sure the dog would come back, even though her puppies were there. Rocky hadn't exactly displayed stellar instincts while having the puppies. But she'd rallied nicely since.

"You knew Seth wouldn't leave that dog to fend for herself," Tom said. "So I guess you weren't too worried, since you didn't do much to persuade him to stay at the cabin."

She might have protested Tom's implicit disapproval. Seth was a grown man and made his own decisions. But it was true she hadn't tried very hard to change Seth's mind about going to Houston with her. And she should have. She should have.

She picked up one of the puppies, the wiggliest, yellowest one, the one she'd been calling Rocky II, and cuddled it close. "Are you about to ask me what my intentions are? Or just point out that he's worth half a dozen of me?"

"At least you realize it." He settled his hat on his head again, but tilted back so that she still saw his face clearly. "Do you also realize how long it's been since he went into a public place like this—" he nodded toward the motel "—if he could avoid it?"

"No." She had to clear her throat. "Since—his accident?" The one he'd never talked about.

"Two years now he's been holed up on that land of his. He hasn't come to Houston to see me, Raz or the folks. He hasn't, as far as I know, stirred past Alpine and Fort Davis, where people have gotten used to the way his face looks."

"There's nothing wrong with how his face looks!" She blinked fiercely, thinking of the bathroom without a mirror. "He's a beautiful man. Maybe he can't see that, but anyone with any sense must."

Tom nodded slowly, as if her outburst had confirmed something. "Those scars don't bother you at all, do they?" Instead of looking pleased, though, he looked tired and sad as he straightened. "Do you know a woman named Linda Haviston? I think she might run with the sort of crowd you grew up with."

An alarm went off in Sophie's head. "A tall brunette with a Lauren Bacall voice?"

"And money," he said. "Don't forget those pots of money her daddy's going to leave her one of these days."

"I don't know her well," Sophie said uneasily. "Why do you ask?"

"She and Seth were engaged at the time of his accident. She sent him roses in the hospital. She even came to see him a couple of times. She just couldn't stand to look at him."

Sophie felt intense anger at the woman who'd hurt Seth, and continued wariness toward Tom Rasmussin. "Why are you telling me this?"

"Linda wasn't cruel. Just weak. Seth's accident changed him in more ways than the obvious, and she couldn't deal with the damage.'' Tom resettled his hat in its usual concealing position. ''You're not like Linda about the scars, but I'm not convinced you're different from her otherwise. She didn't leave him because of the burns, you know. She left because he refused to get plastic surgery.''

Sophie gaped at Tom. He gave her a steady, impenetrable look, then turned and walked away.

She hardly noticed. She was too busy trying to figure out why a man who seemed to hate his scars so much would refuse to have anything done about them.

Seven

Their rooms were pleasant enough, in a generically motel fashion. Seth wondered what they looked like to Sophie, who must be used to much grander accommodations. He didn't ask.

They settled Rocky and the pups in Sophie's room, then brought in suitcases. Seth set his on the luggage rack and glanced at the connecting door. It was closed.

He faced his cousin. "I have some questions."

"All right, but keep it brief." Tom set his canvas tote on the bed. "I need to call Carrasco."

Naturally Tom had to let his captain know he was bringing in a witness. The fact that Tom dealt with Sophie in terms of his case shouldn't have soured Seth's stomach. Tom's job had always been important to him; since the death of his young wife three years ago, it had pretty well taken over his life. "How are you connected with the investigation into the death of Sophie's sister? An accidental overdose doesn't normally rate the attention of Special Investigations.''

"Technically, Christine Cochran didn't overdose." Tom pulled his shaving kit from the tote and crossed to the bathroom. "The stress the drug put on her heart wouldn't have killed her if she hadn't had a previously unsuspected weakness.''

"That doesn't answer my question.''

"I can say this much." Tom faced him. "Farquhar wasn't a pusher. He was far enough up in a certain local organization to be interesting, a couple of rungs below a man named Tyburn Madison. Farquhar had been under observation for some time before Christine Cochran died, so when Sophia Cochran made noises about setting up a sting, we wanted to quiet her down fast. She got passed up to me, but it isn't technically my case, or even HPD's. The feds are running this show, and it's Madison they want. Special Investigations is mostly a liaison between HPD and the two federal agencies involved.''

Whatever Sophie had gotten herself caught up in was big, then. A lot bigger than one death or one drug dealer. The hair on Seth's nape stood up. "How much danger is she in?''

"I hope to God she's lying about her memory, because I don't think she killed Farquhar. I think the man's boss took him out when he became too unstable. Tyburn Madison has a very tidy, very permanent way of handling threats. Threats,'' Tom finished grimly, "like your Sophie.''

Cities made Seth raw. San Antonio was no exception. By the time he got back from gassing up the truck, carrying the pizzas the three of them had agreed on for supper, his nerves were jumping. Maybe someday he'd get used to it—the startled glances, averted eyes, the pool of silence that followed him as conversations paused in his wake . . . the pity.

God knows, he told himself as he grabbed the pizza boxes, if he'd occasionally fallen victim to the sin of vanity in the past, he was paying for it now.

When he reached the top of the stairs he saw Sophie standing in the doorway to his room, frowning up at Tom. Maybe it was the look in Tom's eyes, or the way he stood a little too close. Cop intimidation tactics, Seth told himself, but it didn't help. Jealousy gut-punched him, rolling over him in a wave that crested, then ebbed, making his voice hard. "What's going on?"

Sophie looked at him. She didn't smile. "Detective Rasmussin wants to ask me some more questions. I insisted on waiting for you. I think you deserve to hear whatever answers I've got."

Seth's response to seeing Tom and Sophie together confused him. As bad as things got between himself and Linda, even at the end, when he had every reason for jealousy, he hadn't reacted that way to the sight of her with another man.

"You're right," he said curtly. "But Tom has waited this long. He can hold off until after supper."

Seth started to go into his room, but Sophie's hand on his arm stopped him. Tom gave the two of them one quick, comprehensive glance and went in, though Seth noticed he didn't close the door.

"Seth . . ." Her hand dropped.

He waited, unmoving.

"Why did you come with me?"

He had no intention of trying to explain what he didn't understand himself. "It seemed like the right thing to do."

Her face was pale and strained and stubborn. "You shouldn't have come, Seth. And I shouldn't have let you. I'm sorry . . . for everything."

Behind her words trailed a silence full of implications. He was pretty sure she didn't intend to let him close again—in bed or out of it. Her defenses had returned along with her memory, and she was too smart to get involved with a man like him.

Except that she was already involved. Seth, who knew he wasn't smart at all, didn't intend to let her forget it. Or him.

Maybe it had been a mistake, Sophie thought, to wait for Seth. She didn't want to make trouble for him with his family, yet that's what she was doing. Seth was protective, and his cousin was . . . well, suspicious. The two men had already argued over whether Seth should be allowed to sit in on an official interrogation. Seth had agreed to remain silent, as long as Tom didn't browbeat his witness.

So many mistakes. She sighed as she sat at the round table in her bedroom, twin to the one that still held remnants of pizza in the adjoining room. "Where do we start?"

"With names." Tom set a tape recorder on the table between them and opened his notebook. "I want to know everyone you've ever seen associate with Farquhar."

Tension gripped her body like a familiar, abusive lover. "I have some names from my . . . investigation. I'm almost sure—"

"We'll get to that. I want to start further back."

Tom Rasmussin went "further back," all right, all the way to the year she'd spent with Charles after her parents died. The next three hours were rough. She'd known that speaking of Charles in front of Seth would be hard, and it was. She'd been such a fool. But Seth deserved to know about her. He needed to know.

The worst part was revisiting the time surrounding Christine's death. Tendrils of that wild, guilt-ridden grief tried to pull her under. But she did get to tell Tom about her suspicions of a couple of people from her set she thought were involved with Farquhar's drug dealing. She also told him about a third man she'd seen with Charles, a man she thought was important: ". . . cleanly drawn features with a high forehead. He had white hair and his skin was red, like he had a permanent sunburn, and it had the ironed look of a face-lift."

"Where did you see them together?"

"I saw him with Charles at a restaurant once, then again at Charles's house about a month ago. I can get you the date after we reach Houston. I kept a journal."

"Did you hear their conversation?"

"No, Charles made an excuse to send me out of the room." She leaned forward. "Charles acted odd that day. Not just because he didn't introduce me—he enjoyed being rude sometimes, so that didn't mean anything. But Charles deferred to this man. He seemed . . . I don't know. Maybe afraid."

Seth spoke for the first time in two hours—to his cousin, not Sophie. "Is he the one you told me about?"

Tom sighed. "Sounds like it." He looked squarely at Sophie. "Your description matches that of a man named Tyburn Madison. Farquhar had every reason to fear him. He's the local kingpin in the drug cartel we're investigating and was Farquhar's boss, a man we've been trying to get something on for years."

She gaped. "You already know about him? Then why— you've been asking me questions for hours—"

"I hoped you might have something solid on Madison, something that wasn't hidden in that reluctant memory of yours, maybe something you weren't aware you knew. That's why we started so far back."

"You knew." She was dazed with the discovery of her own futility. "When I came to you and offered to help you trap Farquhar, you already knew all about him."

"Yes, ma'am." Briefly Tom's craggy features softened with what looked like sympathy. "I tried to talk you out of pursuing him on your own."

"You didn't tell me—"

"I couldn't."

So the dangerous course she'd pursued after Christine's death had been worse than foolhardy—it had been useless. Her one solid discovery had been the description of a man the police had known about all along. She looked down, desperately wanting to hold on to enough dignity not to break down. "I guess I was a—what's the expression? A loose cannon in your investigation. A real problem."

"A bit of one, anyway."

The ragged ends of the past grated inside her like a poorly set bone. She rubbed her temple, where a headache was starting. "I understand why you couldn't tell me about your investigation. I was . . . not very reasonable at the time. I wanted Charles Farquhar punished—caught and exposed for the kind of man he was. I wanted that badly. But I didn't kill him."

"Have you remembered anything more about that night?"

Was his question an honest one? Had he decided to believe her? "No."

Of course he couldn't leave it at that. He took her through the night of the party in exhaustive detail, but her memory still stopped at the point when Charles came back after using the phone.

"Tell me exactly what he said."

"I've told you!" she cried, worn-out from recalling that night and the person she'd been then, frightened and angry and tight with purpose.

"Tell me again."

Sophie took a deep breath and slid into the past, seeing it, hearing it.

The room had been chilly in spite of the crowd. Cissy always turned the thermostat too low for anyone but penguins. Sophie had been talking to Melanie Sotheby, who'd overdone the Chanel No. 5, and Sophie's temples had begun to throb with a headache. Excess was all these people understood—too much air-conditioning and alcohol, too much perfume, money and laughter. Then Charles returned from taking a phone call. He smiled at her with absentminded sweetness.

Sophie was only partially aware of the present, of the police detective across the table from her and the man beside her. "He said, 'sorry, sugar, but business calls. See if you can't catch a ride with someone, would you?' He was worried. I could tell." The very sweetness of his expression had given him away. When worried or preoccupied, Charles had always fallen back on the bashful sweetness that charmed young girls, old women, anyone who didn't know his reputation. "That's when I knew..."

"Knew what?" Tom asked softly.

"That it was my chance."

"Your chance for what?"

"I..." For a second, incongruously, an image of the bag of white powder that still rested in Seth's cupboard flashed through her mind. Along with it came the same unexplained weight of guilt she'd felt when she first saw it. "To identify his supplier, I guess."

"You guess? You don't know?"

"That's where my memory stops." Her head pounded dully. "Look, I'm tired, and I really don't think there's any further to take this."

Tom studied her out of unblinking eyes. His gaze didn't soothe her like Seth's did. It made her feel cold and wary. "All right," he said, standing and shutting off the tape recorder. "It's late, and we have a lot of driving ahead of us tomorrow. But we're not finished."

She was afraid that was all too true.

"It would be a good idea to leave the connecting door between our rooms open, Miss Cochran. Just in case."

Just in case she was guilty of murder and tried to make a run for it? Or in case someone was trying to murder her? She shivered.

Seth stood as soon as Tom left. He smiled at her, but she saw the strain around his eyes. He drifted his fingers along the side of her head. "Remember," he said, "that we're not finished either, you and I."

The click of a closing door woke Seth. Or maybe he'd been dozing, not fully asleep, because he knew right away what the sound was—the door to Sophie's room had just shut behind her.

Not a thread of light disturbed the blackness of the motel room. Seth glanced at the glowing red numerals of the clock that sat on the table between the two beds: 2:23.

She wasn't heading out for an early breakfast at this hour. Seth threw his covers back and sat up, reaching for his jeans.

"I'll get her." Tom's voice came from the other bed, along with the same sort of bed-creaking, clothes-rustling sounds Seth made as he pulled on his jeans.

"No." Seth pulled up the zipper.

"She's my witness. If she's making a run for it—"

"I guess suspicion comes naturally to a cop." Seth felt his way around the bed, heading for the door. "But give it a rest, will you?"

"You're not suspicious? Then why are you racing after her so damned fast?"

Seth opened the door to the hall without answering.

The metal pickup bed was cool and dirty. The rush of cars along the nearby interstate was a sour mockery of the rush of wind through the pines back on Seth's mountain. Sophie leaned against the curving part of the bed that went over one rear wheel, her head tilted back to look at the stars. But the stars weren't clear here. City haze overlay the clean darkness like a gauzy scarf.

When she heard the footsteps she didn't move. She knew who it was. "I tried not to wake anyone."

The pickup dipped as Seth swung up over the tailgate. He didn't speak until he settled next to her. "Tom doesn't really think you killed Farquhar, you know. He considers it part of his job to act suspicious."

"Does he?" Slowly she straightened. "He cares about you. He doesn't want you to get hurt."

"Am I going to be hurt?"

"I hope not," she whispered. "Seth, I—"

He took her hand, lacing his fingers through hers. "Are you going to apologize again?"

Her faint smile surprised her. "I think so."

"Resist the urge."

She didn't answer, and for a while they just sat there together. The pickup bed didn't make a very comfortable seat. It was uneven, and the humped part over the wheel was too low to lean against properly. After a minute she shifted, pulling her hand back to wrap her arms around her upraised knees.

He released her hand easily. "I guess it's pretty strange to lose yourself so completely, and then have everything come back at once."

"The strange part," she said, staring out at the lights whizzing by on the interstate, "is that I feel more lost now than I did yesterday, when I didn't know who I was."

"You didn't want to remember."

"No." She sighed. "I told you I might not like myself very much."

Headlights flashed and laughter followed as a car of late-night merrymakers zigzagged its way across the parking lot. Sophie had given up on getting a response from Seth, when he spoke. "Even before you remembered, you told me that your sister's death was your fault. Nothing I've heard fits that."

"How can you say that?" The car staggered to a halt aslant a couple of spaces, and its doors opened, spilling its drunken contents from both sides. One woman called to the other in Spanish, and everyone laughed. The women's laughter sounded shrill and stupid to Sophie. "Weren't you paying attention when your cousin questioned me? Look."

She sat forward, gesturing at the people who talked and laughed too loudly as they crossed the parking lot. "That's *me*, Seth. That's how I acted, how I looked, a few years ago. Oh, I probably got out of a Jaguar instead of a Ford— what's the difference? I drank too much. I partied too much. I let a man like Charles use me. That's the kind of example I set for my sister at a time when she needed me most, after our parents died. Is it any wonder she wouldn't listen to me when I told her Charles was bad news?''

''Let's see if I understand.'' Seth brought his leg up and rested his arm on his knee. ''You and your parents had been unusually close, and you went a little crazy when they died. Blew your grade point average all to hell in your senior year but managed to graduate anyway. Then you got involved with Farquhar, started partying, and you slept with everything in pants.''

Sophie felt the blood drain from her face. ''No! It wasn't—I didn't—''

''Didn't sleep around?'' His voice was deceptively soft in the partial darkness. ''So that's not what's bothering you. It must be the drinking. Are you an alcoholic?''

She blinked, surprised and a little hurt. ''No.''

''How about drugs? You told Tom you didn't use them, that Farquhar wasn't yet into the drug scene when you two were together. Was that a lie? Do you still have a habit? Is that where Christine got the idea of taking drugs?''

''No, of course not! I don't know what you're trying to prove, but—''

''Then maybe you weren't telling the truth when you said you broke off with Farquhar's crowd when you broke off with him. That was—what? Three, four years ago? So you feel responsible for Christine's bad choices because your friends were such a bad influence on her.''

''No, but—you don't understand.'' Weariness descended, a heavy weight of inadequacy and lost chances. She laid her head on her knees.

''Tell me.''

She wanted to. She wished she had words to describe the slow return of life to parts of her that had been all but dead after a year spent with the shallow, easy-living crowd that Charles Farquhar ran with—used to run with, she corrected herself. Charles was dead.

"I didn't break up with Charles," she said quietly. "He dumped me. That's been one of the hardest things for me to accept. I not only let myself be seduced by that bastard, I didn't wake up to what he was until later. Christine didn't believe anything I told her about him. She thought I was bitter toward him because of the way he'd left me, that I was jealous and vindictive. I'm sure that's what Charles told her."

He wrapped his arm around her shoulder and pulled her to him.

She pressed her hands against his chest. "Seth, no."

"Shh." He kept pulling, gently, inexorably. "It's chilly out here, and the cold makes my leg ache. Sit close to me, Sophie, and warm it up."

Warm it up? Was he crazy?

No, she was. Blast the man, how could she not come closer? This was the first time he'd referred, even obliquely, to the damage done to his body. She remembered oh-so-clearly the deceptively neat surgical scar along that muscular calf, remembered running her hand along it when they were naked in bed together....

She sighed and let him gather her up against him. "Why won't you call me Sophia?"

Apparently he wasn't interested in answering her question. "What part of Houston do you live in?"

"River Oaks."

"It figures," he said dryly. "Any house in River Oaks is bound to have plenty of bedrooms. You do realize, don't you, that I'm staying with you once we reach Houston?"

She did want him to stay with her. To stay and stay...she straightened, pulling away from the warmth of him. "No way."

His hand reached out, briefly tracing the healing scrapes on the side of her face. "Someone tried to hurt you. I'm not going to let them try again."

Why couldn't she have met him before? "Listen." She scooted to the tailgate and climbed out. "Obviously I've given you the wrong impression. As much as I appreciate—I mean, once we get to Houston, that's it. You are not staying with me." *Where you would be a target, too.*

He landed on the ground beside her and grabbed her arm. "That's it? Thanks, and goodbye?" He shook his head slowly. "It won't work, Sophie."

"It's because you slept with me, isn't it?" she cried, flushing in the darkness. "That's why you're going to Houston with me. You feel some sort of responsibility toward me because—because of us being together."

"Yes."

She felt as if she'd run into a wall. Winded. Dazed. But not hurt, she told herself. She wasn't hurt that he saw her as an obligation. "Seth." The necessity of explaining left her nauseous. "The person you were with last night doesn't really exist. Not anymore. So your responsibility is ended."

His fingers tightened on her arm. Her eyes widened with surprise a second before he sealed her mouth with his.

When she opened her eyes the world still spun slowly, like a saucer ringing around in circles on its rim before it settled, with a distinctive clink, back into place. She blinked several times, trying to get her breath under control. The hand she'd involuntarily lifted to hold his face to hers fell to her side. And she said, quite clearly, "That's just sex."

His breath came hard like hers, but the light in his eyes looked amazingly like amusement. "You let me know when you're ready to have 'just sex' again, then." He released her arm and walked away.

Houston.

A sprawling megacity with too many cars, too many people, too much crime. Home of the first successful heart transplant and the Houston Oilers, the Galleria and NASA, the Texas Opera Theatre and Astroworld. Seth's home, too, for many years.

But this, Seth thought as they pulled up in the curved driveway in front of the huge, colonial-style home, sure didn't look like Houston Heights, where his aunt and uncle still lived. In the Heights he'd played baseball in the vacant lot on the corner. Kids who grew up in River Oaks played— what? Tennis? Polo?

"Your neighbors are going to worry about what you're doing to the neighborhood," Seth said as he got out of his mud-spattered pickup. An equally dirty Jeep pulled in behind them.

"They already do."

He glanced at her, wondering what she meant by that. "I've got a couple things to take care of once I get unpacked. I won't leave you alone, though. Tom's probably reached Raz on his cellular by now. He'll stay here with you while I'm gone." He opened the door and got out.

"I don't need a sitter." Sophie climbed out of the pickup and ran a hand through the short hair the wind had made a mess of. She stood still for a long moment, staring at the elegant house shaded by oaks and elms and adorned with azaleas that would be beautiful in the spring. "I can remember when this place felt like home," she said at last, "but it doesn't anymore." She shook her head. "Come on. Let's get Rocky and the pups settled."

Seth glanced at the big house, automatically checking exits and accessibility. Why in the world did anyone need three stories? Getting someone off that third floor if there was a fire would be a real bitch. Two stories were bad enough.

He ought to know. His aching knee reminded him of how bad two stories could be as he moved to the back of the truck.

At 7:03 that evening Sophie came out of hiding.

Tom had left almost as soon as they arrived that afternoon. Seth had said something about leaving, too, but she didn't know if he'd actually gone, because she'd avoided him ever since showing him to his room.

She'd told Seth before she escaped that she had to make some phone calls, and it was true. Her few close friends had been worried about her absence, especially after the police went around asking questions. But after calling Maddie and Sarah, her two oldest friends, and talking to Evelyn—her newest friend as well as her boss at the children's home—Sophie had stayed in her room. Hiding.

Having Seth in her house disturbed her. Just being here upset her. Everything she saw carried such a heavy freight of memories. She felt split, sundered, and didn't know how to knit the pieces of herself back together.

Maybe the problem was that she didn't want to be back together. She wanted to be the person she'd been on Seth's mountain, the person, she thought wistfully as she headed down the stairs, she might have become if she'd never met Charles Farquhar. Or if she'd been a little stronger, or wiser, when she met him.

But at 7:02 her housekeeper, Mrs. Porter, had rung her on the in-house line to say that she didn't know how Sophie expected her to get any cooking done with a dog and five puppies underfoot, that dinner would be on the table in twenty minutes, and was "that man at the front of the house" staying for dinner?

As much as Sophie dreaded having to face Seth, her steps grew lighter as she approached the front sitting room, where the movement of a shadow across the arched entry announced his presence. Stupidly, helplessly, she wanted to see him again.

Sophie stepped into the doorway and froze.

There was a man in the room. Not Seth. Sophie stared at the back of the man's head for one frozen second. Longish hair, but a light, tawny brown, *not Seth,* and broad shoulders in a nicely tailored sports jacket—*not Seth!*—and he was turning and would see her in another moment and she backed up quickly—too quickly. She stumbled against the table and knocked her elbow against the frame of the door.

"Ms. Cochran?" the man said, smiling a wide, white smile that fell away when she jumped, ready to run. "No, wait—I'm Raz, Seth's cousin." He reached inside his jacket and pulled out a small leather case, Flipping it open, he crossed to her. "I don't blame you for being jumpy. Have a look."

The case held his police ID. "Lieutenant Ferdinand M. Rasmussin," she read on the shield. "Well," she said, feeling incredibly foolish. "Now I know why they call you Raz."

He ate supper with her. Rocky deserted her pups to join them, begging with great dignity and a cold, wet nose. Raz explained in a friendly, unending flow of words that Seth had gone to make arrangements with a private security firm, who now had men guarding her house. Then he'd gone to have supper with his aunt and uncle.

"Two hired guards aren't enough?" she asked wryly, pushing her green beans around with her fork. Funny how her appetite had left. Funny how she could get her feelings hurt that Seth hadn't told her himself where he was going, and not at all reasonable. She'd closed herself up in her room, for goodness' sake. "He had to ask you to stay with me, too?"

"Four guards, actually," he corrected her cheerfully. "Two out front, two out back. May I?" He served himself another salmon croquette. "This is delicious. Your housekeeper cooks like a dream. I may propose."

As they ate their meal and her guest talked on, both of them sneaking bites to Rocky from time to time, Sophie began to relax. Raz's charm was both practiced and intentional, but it was so very well done. And he was, after all, Seth's cousin, though he looked nothing like Seth, or like his older, harder brother, for that matter.

She asked him about himself, as any good hostess should, and about his family. Seth's family.

Raz didn't seem to mind her delicate probing. Nor did he mistake where her interest lay. He readily offered up those bits of family lore that make up a large part of a person's story. He talked about Seth as a boy. Sophie listened greedily. At the end of the meal he casually mentioned Seth's decision to buy the mountain his cabin sat on.

Sophie set down the fork that had been carrying a bite of pie to her mouth. "He what? He bought the whole mountain?"

"His land covers three or four peaks, actually, along with his valley. You didn't know?"

She shook her head, trying to fit that indication of wealth into the Seth she knew, the man who lived in a log cabin and dressed in work shirts and worn jeans. "I don't understand."

"His parents were insured, and a few years after they died there was a hefty settlement from the company that installed the wiring in their home. Bad wiring caused the fire they died in, you know. He'd never touched any of it before his accident, just let the interest pile up in the mutual fund where my parents invested it for him. I imagine he's almost as well-off as you are, even after buying the land."

She sat motionless, stunned. "A fire? His parents died in a fire?"

"He was spending the night at a friend's house the night of the fire." Raz's charm and humor slid away, giving her a glimpse of a man who wasn't as different from Seth and Tom as she'd thought. "He took their deaths hard. Even at ten he blamed himself, thinking that if he'd been home he could have done something, saved them somehow. I figure that's why he went into fire fighting. He was good at it, maybe too good. He earned all kinds of awards."

"Before the accident."

"Yes."

The assault of Raz's revelations left her feeling winded. And determined. "Why would you say he was 'too good' at fire fighting?"

He met her eyes gravely for a moment. At last he pushed back from the table. "Let's go in the other room. Does that marvelous housekeeper of yours have some coffee made, do you think?''

Of course Mrs. Porter had coffee ready. They took it in the front parlor with them. Sophie gave Raz enough time to sit down and take a sip of coffee before bringing the conversation back to what mattered. ''So. Why was Seth 'too good' at what he did?''

Raz leaned back in the armchair, crossing his legs man-style, with one ankle resting on the opposite knee. ''He got used to winning, to being the best. When he finally lost, and lost big, he tossed out years of training and skill by walking away from fire fighting.''

''He could have stayed with it, even with his injuries?''

''He could have stayed in the same field. A lot of fire marshals and arson investigators were once fire fighters. There's always a need for teachers, too.''

Sophie thought about that for a minute. ''When I asked Seth why he considers the work he does with plants a hobby, he said he couldn't earn a living at it. But it isn't really the lack of money that keeps him from taking his naturalism seriously, is it?''

''No. Not really.''

While they finished their coffee, Raz told Sophie about fire fighting. It was a unique profession, almost addictive. Like police work, fire fighting was made up of long stretches of boredom punctuated by periods of intense stress and intense highs. Unlike police work, the value of the job was usually obvious and immediate. The fire got put out. A building or a family was saved. Intense camaraderie often developed among fire fighters because each individual's life depended on everyone else, uniting fire fighting teams in the same sort of bond that welds fighting units together in wartime.

Seth had been a fire fighter for eight years. What other job, what other sort of life, could offer all that?

Sophie was beginning to understand what Tom had meant when he said that Seth's scars were only the part of the damage that showed, not the most important part. "Will you tell me what happened? How he was hurt?"

"Has he told you anything?"

"No." He'd made love to her, but he didn't trust her with the hurt part of himself, and why should he? She had a record of letting people down. "Before I knew he'd been a fire fighter I'd imagined a lot of things. Some of them," she admitted with a self-conscious smile, "were downright silly. Hollywood stuff. He'd been an agent on a mission, or a bomb expert and things went wrong, or almost anything, I guess, to make whatever happened to him seem more like a story. Less real."

"You needn't feel ashamed of that."

Raz had a comfortable voice, private yet neutral, a voice that invited confidences. Sophie relaxed against the sofa and tucked one foot up under her. It was nice, she thought, that at least one of Seth's cousins didn't despise her. "I . . . have a tendency to hide from unpleasantness." An understatement, that. Losing her memory so she could hide even from herself was the most drastic example of that weakness, but the pattern had been laid down early. Her parents couldn't have kept her so happily ignorant of life's realities if she hadn't been willing not to see the ugliness. "I'm trying to change."

"Have you considered asking Seth about the accident?"

She shook her head. "He doesn't even have a mirror in his house. How can I ask him to talk about something that hurts him so much?"

"Well," he said, "Seth was always a bit vain."

She stiffened in shock.

He chuckled at her expression and set his cup and saucer down. "I'm not quite the callous bastard that you're thinking. But Seth . . . he was born pretty, you see."

He leaned forward, his elbows on his spread knees. "My mom says people used to stop Seth's mother on the street to fuss over her beautiful baby, even a Hollywood talent scout, once. They turned down that offer and a couple of others because they didn't want him to grow up depending on his looks. Still, he stayed cute. Girls sighed after him. By the time he got to high school he should have been impossibly conceited, yet somehow all the attention didn't ruin him. But he was human. He knew what effect his looks had on others, especially women. He couldn't help but like it.''

"And then it was gone," she said slowly. And not just gone. The flattering glow of approval in people's eyes would have turned, overnight, into horror. Pity. Or both.

His fiancée had left him. Right after the accident, when the damage was at its worst and he was the most vulnerable, people's reactions would have seared nearly as deeply as the flames...flames from some real fire, not a special effects spectacular that made you hold your breath as you waited for the hero to come out of the burning barn, untouched.

Unconsciously seeking comfort, she brought her knees up and hugged them to her. "A house fire...that's probably the most common, isn't it? I thought about that before we left his mountain." When she lay in his arms that night and couldn't sleep. "His cabin doesn't have any interior walls, and I thought about how someone who'd once been caught in a fire wouldn't want walls in his home to slow him down if he had to get out in a hurry. Walls that might trap him."

"I hadn't thought about that. You're right, though, the lack of walls in his cabin is important. But it was Seth's parents who were trapped when their house burned, not him. Seth was hurt in a house fire, too, but not that way. He was at one of the upper-floor windows when the flashover hit him."

"Flashover?" she repeated, a tightness crawling up her chest.

"Sometimes, with a very hot fire nearby, everything in an area reaches ignition point at once, including the combustible gasses collected at ceiling level. The fire flashes out over the entire area almost instantaneously."

Her breath caught. She saw it, saw the exploding fireball that leapt out and burned Seth, hurting him forever. She closed her eyes and still saw it. After a moment another feeling penetrated the horrific vision.

Anger. She was angry with him. He was a hero. Hadn't she, in her juvenile imaginings, known that about him? She hated that he'd risked himself, hurt himself trying to save someone's home, making himself into the sort of man she could never hope to deserve.

She blinked back tears that came from too many emotions, none of them simple.

Seth's cousin looked straight at her then, and once more she saw the resemblance. Raz's eyes weren't as dark as Seth's, but there was something in the shape, the expression... "Ask him," he said. "If you want to know about the accident, ask Seth. He's hiding, too."

Eight

The stained glass window at the landing would be colorful in the daytime, Seth thought as he headed slowly down the white marble staircase, his knee throbbing in rhythm with his steps. But darkness had fallen some time ago, and the colors of the glass had died back to their nighttime obscurity.

It had been a long day. Sophie had done a quick fade right after showing him his room that afternoon. She'd claimed the need to let some people know she was all right after being gone for days. Seth didn't doubt that was true. He also didn't doubt she'd used it as a reason to hide from him.

He accepted that, for now. He'd had a lot to get done, anyway, that afternoon. He'd gone to North Security, then to police headquarters.

Then, for the first time in nearly two years, he'd gone to see his aunt and uncle.

There wasn't much color in the elegant foyer at the foot of the stairs, either. A rug by the door matched the silvery veining in the marble stairs and floor. The noncolor was picked up again in the runner that covered the center of the stairs, held in place by wrought iron rods at each step. Not unattractive, Seth thought as he stepped onto the chilly marble floor. But the formal style didn't look like Sophie to him.

Of course, the only time he'd seen her wearing her own clothes, she'd been battered, unconscious, with her clothes in slightly worse shape than she was. So maybe he didn't really know much about her style.

The door to the study stood open. Seth went in.

Tom sat in one of the two big armchairs in front of the desk, where a crystal decanter sat on a silver tray. His feet were propped up on a leather hassock, displaying the worn soles of his cowboy boots. He lifted a glass of amber liquor in salute. "Raz told me I'd like the housekeeper here. She knows how to take care of a man."

A smile tugged at Seth's mouth. Mrs. Porter was a dour, disagreeable woman with heavy jowls and no ankles—her legs were equally thick from the calves down to her sensibly shod feet. "I'm glad you didn't mind waiting for me." He lowered himself carefully into the other armchair. His knee had stiffened up over the long drive, and the shower he'd just taken hadn't done much to ease it.

"Here." Tom tossed a file folder in Seth's lap.

Seth glanced at it. The label at the top of the file read Tyburn Madison. "Thanks." Seth's fingers tightened on the manila folder. It would be heavily edited, he knew. Tom had warned him of that when Seth persuaded him to make a copy of the police file on Madison that afternoon. But Seth needed to learn as much as he could about the man who wanted Sophie dead. He'd take what he could get.

"I saw one of North's men out front," Tom said, taking another sip. "You make the arrangements?"

"There are two men out front, actually, with another pair around back. North suggested two teams of two men each, relieved every eight hours, until he can have a look at Sophie's security system to see what needs beefing up. I told him to go for it. She can afford it.''

Tom swirled the liquor and melting ice in his glass lazily. ''That bother you? Her money?''

Seth stretched out an arm and snagged the other glass and the decanter. ''Not really.'' The lid on the decanter was a huge, leaded glass teardrop. Subtle rainbows hid inside. ''There's no reason for her money to be an issue between us. It isn't as if I'm marrying her, after all.''

''I see. You just want to sleep with her. She must be damned good in bed to get you down off your mountain.''

''Dammit!'' Seth's fingers tightened around the decanter. Deliberately he relaxed them, and poured. ''I'm in no mood for you to rattle my cage tonight, Tom.''

Tom sipped at his drink again, watching Seth over the rim of the glass. ''Do you think she'll agree to try hypnosis?''

''I don't know why not.''

''Maybe because she's lying about not remembering. Maybe because she doesn't really want the killer caught.''

''Come on. Someone tried to kill her and she doesn't want them stopped?''

''You didn't see her three months ago in my office, insisting we use her in a sting against Farquhar. I thought I talked her out of it. Instead, she set out to do it herself.'' Tom shook his head. ''When a person's obsessed with vengeance, there's no telling where they'll draw the line. She might be grateful to whoever killed Farquhar.''

Three months. Seth rubbed his face wearily, his fingers lingering over the different texture on the left side. He hadn't realized her sister's death was so recent. ''Grief doesn't make a basically decent person go out and commit murder. Or sanction murder.''

''I don't think she killed Farquhar. That doesn't mean she's told me everything.''

No, she hadn't. Neither had Seth, but it was time to take care of that, now that they were a few hundred miles away from the evidence. ''There's something you need to know.''

Seth's tone of voice must have alerted his cousin. Tom leaned forward, tensing. "What?"

"When I went through Sophie's things the night I found her, there was a plastic bag of white powder in one of her pockets. Two or three ounces, I'd say. It's at the cabin still."

Tom slammed his glass down and sprang to his feet. For a minute Seth thought his cousin was going to swing at him. Instead he cursed steadily, finishing with, "I damned well ought to lock you up for withholding evidence!"

"What the hell do you think you could have done with the bag if I'd given it to you? You couldn't have gotten fingerprints on that surface. You couldn't have traced it. You'd probably have arrested her for possession, and what would that have accomplished?"

"If I had her in jail, I wouldn't have to worry about someone taking potshots at her." A muscle jumped in Tom's cheek. "Oh, hell." He ran a hand over his hair, front to back. "Maybe this explains what happened to those blasted peekaboo memories of hers."

"What do you mean?"

"If she's been using, as part of her effort to trap Farquhar—"

"She's not on drugs."

"I'm sure she hasn't had a chance to get to any while at your cabin, but that doesn't mean she wasn't using before."

Seth spaced his words slowly, for emphasis. "Sophie does not, and has not, used cocaine."

"How would you know, for God's sake?"

"Because she told me."

"Dammit, Seth, would you listen to yourself?" Tom paced a few steps away. "You've only known her for what, seven days? And she wasn't in her right mind most of the time, if her story about this off-again, on-again memory of hers is true—"

"It's true."

"You do realize you're not making any sense, don't you? You don't *know* this woman, Seth."

"I suppose you do?"

"Hell, no, but I'm aware of it, at least. You seem to think you know everything about her, when you didn't even know her last name until I showed up! She can't be that damned good a—"

"Enough!" Seth shoved to his feet. "You think I don't know what your problem is?"

"It isn't me with the problem."

"No? You want her so damn bad you can't see straight. Hell, you probably having trouble walking straight. And you hate it. You haven't wanted anything to make you feel alive since Allison died. Maybe you hate me, too. Because I've got Sophie, and I'm not letting her go."

For long, strained seconds Tom didn't answer. His pale eyes gave little away, but his silence did. Slowly he moved to the desk. His black Stetson lay there, brim up. He picked it up. "*Hate* would be too strong a word. We're family. That hasn't changed." He settled the hat on his head. "But don't be too sure about what you've got, when you're not willing to back it up in the way that matters to a woman." He turned and walked out.

Seth watched him go. His knee ached relentlessly, and he wondered just how much he would end up paying for his time with Sophie. Surely his relationship with Tom was too high a price.

But he couldn't let her go. Not yet. With a sigh, he lowered himself back into the chair, grimacing at the way the ache was spreading. He grabbed the glass of Scotch he'd poured but not tasted and tossed it down. The quick-fire burn of it shocked his system awake, and he picked up the file Tom had brought.

First things first. Stopping Tyburn Madison had to come ahead of everything else. He started reading.

* * *

Pamela C. Dean's *The Secret Country*. Katherine Kurtz's *Deryni* books. The *Belgariad* series by David Eddings—and Tolkien's books. Unlike the others, they were bound in expensive leather. Sophie could barely read the titles in the dim, early-morning light, but she knew them. She remembered.

The fingers of her left hand lingered on the stamped leather binding of *The Hobbit*. This wasn't her original set of Tolkien, which had been in paperback. Her father had given her this set when she was fifteen. Usually Sophie's mother had done the gift buying, but her father had always picked out one present personally for his daughters. That year, the year she turned fifteen, Sophie's mother had given her a new saddle for Trixie, her quarter horse, and a pile of pretty clothes. Her father gave her Tolkien. She'd been so smug when she pulled the paper off, because she'd guessed what his present was that year, and she'd been right.

The memory hurt. She felt rather like a voyager who's returned home from a long trip. Everything was familiar, and yet she saw it all with new eyes. Memories lay everywhere, and the good ones were as painful in some ways as the bad.

Sophie lowered herself to the floor in front of the wall of bookcases. *It's a pity,* she thought as she sat Indian-style, *that I let Christine talk me into removing the rug here in Papa's reading room. The wooden floor is really too hard—*

Christine. Sophie closed her eyes as a bolt of fresh grief pierced her. That pain wasn't far enough in the past to have acquired the bittersweet patina of her memories of her parents. Her recent memories of Christine were abrupt and jarring. Within three months of her first date with Farquhar, the shy girl with the soft voice had disappeared, replaced by a shrill, brittle teenager who pulled further and further into herself as her affair continued.

Sophie preferred her earlier memories, of a young girl as blond as Sophie was herself, with identically pale eyebrows and lashes. A girl a little too withdrawn after their parents died. A little too needy. Christine had needed so much, more than Sophie had possessed herself, or knew how to give, so much that eventually she became easy prey for Charles.

If Charles hadn't decided to take advantage of that neediness, someone else would have.

The thought startled Sophie. Was it true? Would Christine have found another man who wanted to use her if Sophie's former lover hadn't come sniffing around?

The door opened. Sophie wasn't at all surprised to see Seth standing there.

If Sophie had thought that seeing him here in the civilized setting of her parents' home would diminish the pull, she knew now she'd been wrong. The city took nothing away from him. His shoulders still strained the seams of his blue shirt. He wore his too-long hair tied back, and his jeans tight. It was, she decided, as if a piece of the mountain's wilderness had followed her home. Slowly she stood. "I was going to come looking for you in a little while."

"Were you?" He started across the room toward her.

She nodded. "I have to learn not to hide from what frightens me. I—" She put out her hand as he came close, too close. It couldn't have been the light pressure of her fingers that stopped him, yet he stopped. "I have responsibilities. Yesterday I let myself avoid them."

"What responsibilities, Sophie?"

What he did to her name made a shiver run up her spine. She stiffened it. "At the West Houston Home for Children. I'm the program director." Evelyn had told her she didn't need to come in today, or tomorrow either. But Sophie knew how shorthanded they were. She knew, too, that the kids didn't need to have an adult they'd grown to count on suddenly disappear.

"You have a job?"

She tried not to bristle at the surprise in his voice. "Not a paid job. That would be ridiculous when I have no need for the salary." Especially since she paid for a large part of the home's expenses herself. "I'm a volunteer, but that doesn't reduce the importance of the commitment."

Half of his mouth smiled. "Am I being a jerk?" He raised his hand, rested it alongside her cheek. His thumb stroked lightly, sending ribbons of fire spinning out from the delicate contact. "Sophie, you can't go to the home today."

"What?" She pulled back.

"Someone tried to kill you," he said patiently. "I've arranged for as much protection as I can, but it isn't safe to go wandering around Houston."

"Houston," she said dryly, "has never been safe. I told you, Seth. I have to stop hiding."

"Does that mean you're going to stop hiding from this, too?" As slowly and inevitably as fate, his arms went around her. Without pressure, without force, he drew her closer, though he left an agonizing inch of space between their bodies. Her breath stopped. She tilted her head up.

Seth's eyes were filled with darkness, the darkness of the mountain sky at night, clean and endless. The darkness of the unseen, of wind and ghosts and feelings . . . of a man's hunger for a woman.

Her breath started again raggedly. His eyelids lowered, and he bent his head.

"Seth . . . ?"

His lips brushed hers. Warm.

"Are you trying to—change my mind about going to the home?" Her hands rested on his chest.

"Yes."

With an effort, she turned her face away. So he kissed her cheek, her brow line. "It won't work," she managed to say, but her hand now clutched at his shirt, and his feathery kisses excited a reaction as hidden as it was violent. "And it isn't fair to you. My life is such a mess . . ."

"Too late. I'm already in your life, Sophie."

She took a breath, wanting to explain to him, hoping to clear some of the dizziness away, but somehow her face was tipped up to his again and his mouth once more touched hers. Once—

"It's all right, Sophie," he murmured, while his arms tightened, bringing her fully, snugly against him.

Twice—

"Like you told me," he whispered into her mouth while the languid heat wrapped itself around her and her neck wilted, letting her head drop onto his shoulder, "it's just sex. Right?"

Three times.

His mouth stopped teasing, and took. Sophie's brain spun off, and her body, her needs, took over. Her arms wrapped around him as fiercely as his did around her, and she offered him everything she was so desperate to receive.

Later she would be irritated that Seth had heard the door open when she'd been unable to hear, see or think. All she knew then was that his mouth left hers, and his hands put her carefully at a distance.

As Mrs. Porter's disapproving voice penetrated Sophie's fogged brain, she managed to turn around.

"... another policeman here. You might tell him I've better things to do than answer the door at this ungodly early hour. The maid doesn't get here before nine, you know." Mrs. Porter paused, looked at the two of them sternly and shook her head.

"A policeman?" Sophie gulped in air, hoping it would clear her head. "Does this policeman have a name, Mrs. Porter?"

"Certainly," Raz said from the hall. "As you could see for yourself if your handmaiden, here, would move out of the way."

A giggle surprised Sophie by wiggling its way out. "My what?"

"Police," Mrs. Porter muttered as she did, indeed, step aside. "It's not what I expected when I came here, that's for sure, police coming around day after day, ringing the bell before decent folks are out, staying underfoot..." Her complaints faded down the hall along with her broad, retreating back.

Raz came into the room. "She makes the word *police* sound a lot like *cockroaches,* doesn't she?" He didn't grin, quite, as he looked at the two of them, but his expression made it clear he'd seen the embrace his arrival had put an end to.

Seth's arm still rested around her waist. She was acutely conscious of that as he spoke to his cousin. "You're out and about early."

"That's how it is with us vermin," Raz said cheerfully. "Turn out the lights and we come crawling out of the walls. Is your housekeeper an old family retainer?" he asked Sophie, one eyebrow lifting.

"Not exactly." A laugh worked its way out. Maybe she should have been embarrassed at being caught in a passionate clinch, but all she felt was relief. Apparently this cousin didn't object to her involvement with Seth the way the other one did. "Not at all, actually. I hope you'll overlook her odd manners and stay for breakfast. My handmaiden may not sound very welcoming, but she takes pride in doing her job well. I imagine she's already set a place for you."

"All right, then. Thank you. But I really came by to have a word with my cousin, and to discuss your situation."

Her "situation." She grimaced. "So this is an official visit?"

"In part." He slanted Seth an unreadable look. "I should explain, first, that I'm not directly involved with this case, so the request I'm about to make is unofficial. But I hope you'll consider it carefully. Tom thinks, and I agree, that it's your best way of dealing with the threat to your life posed by Tyburn Madison."

Well. That was blunt enough. "Go on."

"The department has a therapist on staff who is experienced with hypnosis. That may be the fastest way to get to these memories of—"

"No." Her heart jammed in her throat. She put a hand there, feeling the pulse jump around crazily. "No, I don't want to be hypnotized."

He paused. "Do you want to tell me why?"

She didn't know why. She just knew the idea made her skin crawl. "Being hypnotized...it sounds like something that would be done *to* me. A sort of voluntary helplessness."

When Seth's big hands went to her shoulders, she jumped. He ignored that, turning her to face him. "Being hypnotized won't make you a victim, Sophie."

She wriggled her shoulders, trying to free herself. "I don't like the idea."

"Do you like the idea of being a target for Madison?"

"I'll be a target anyway! If I remember and testify against him, or if I don't remember, and he doesn't believe I don't remember. Either way, I'm a threat. Unless enough time goes by that he can see I'm not going to give evidence against him. Then maybe he'll leave me alone."

Raz spoke. "Men like Madison don't think that way. As long as you're alive, you're a threat."

She shivered.

"Sophie," Seth said very softly, "I thought you were going to stop hiding."

She stared up at him, trapped, and suddenly aware of one reason she hated the idea of being hypnotized.

She'd lose Seth. She didn't know how, or why, but she felt certain that if she did what Seth asked of her, she'd lose him. "I'll think about it. That's all I can promise, to think about it. Now," she said, moving back so that his hands fell from her shoulders, "shall we go see how many places Mrs. Porter set for breakfast?"

An awkward pause fell. Raz broke it. "Do you think your Valkyrie would be offended if Seth and I are a little late coming to the table? I need to talk with him for a minute."

Sophie knew when she'd been politely dismissed. She looked from one to the other of the men, wondering what they needed privacy to discuss. "I imagine I can restrain her for a little while, but don't be too late, gentlemen. Or I'll send her after you." With a mixture of relief and frustrated curiosity, she left them to their secrets.

Seth watched the door close behind Sophie before facing his cousin. "I expected to see Tom here this morning. Has Vice gotten dragged into this case along with everyone else?" With two federal agencies along with HPD Special Investigations there were already too many people to keep track of.

"No, we're not. Like I said, I'm not officially connected to the case. I came as a favor to Tom."

"I see." Seth turned away to stare out the window. The gray of early morning was brightening to the mellow gold of an autumn day. "It's not like him to let . . . personal considerations affect the way he does his job."

"He thought I'd have a better chance of persuading her to try the hypnosis than he would. Apparently he's been less than charming with Ms. Cochran. Unfortunately," Raz finished with disgust, "I blew it."

"It wasn't you."

"Maybe." He let a pause fall. "He said to tell you there's no word of a contract being out on her."

Seth's eyes closed in relief. After reading Madison's file, that question had plagued him. The man certainly had the contacts and the money to get professional "help" with the problem Sophie posed. "Maybe we're wrong about how serious Madison is about getting rid of her."

"I'm afraid it's more likely that he intends to handle it locally, with his own people."

Fear closed in like smoke, trying to cut off his breath. Seth shoved it back deliberately. "She has a better chance if the talent's local, doesn't she?"

"Probably. A real pro is damned hard to stop." Raz pulled his cigarettes out of his pocket, looked at them and pulled one out. "She needs to try the hypnosis, Seth."

"I'll get her to agree." Somehow. Seth supposed that learning that whoever had tried to kill Sophie was probably not a professional hit man had to be called good news. But good news sure came in hard-to-read shades of gray sometimes. He inhaled deeply, working his way out of the clinging fear. "She's right that testifying against Madison isn't necessarily going to stop him. What the hell is the department doing about him?"

"I don't know. No, calm down, I'm not in a need-to-know position on this. But I can tell you Tom didn't send me here just because he's avoiding you. He's in a meeting right now with Carrasco, the Chief, a DEA honcho for this region, and someone from an agency us peons aren't supposed to know anything about." Raz turned the cigarette over in his hands a couple times, shrugged and put it back in the pack. He looked directly at Seth. "He's doing everything he can, Seth. And not just for your sake."

"I know."

"Do you?" Raz tucked the cigarettes back in his pocket. "He's not doing it for Sophie, either. Or not a hundred percent for her. Have you noticed how much she looks like Allison?"

Seth frowned as he thought about the pretty, petite woman Tom had married. Allison's eyes had been blue, not green like Sophie's, and her features had been more delicate, but Sophie's soft blond hair and her build were nearly identical to the dead woman's. "Damn."

Raz slanted him a questioning look. "Do you think she's like Allison in any way other than superficially?"

Seth knew what he was asking. Tom's wife had been lovely, loving...and fragile. Seth had always privately thought that one reason Allison's condition had gone downhill so fast after the cancer was diagnosed was that she just wasn't a fighter.

Sophie, on the other hand, had reacted to her sister's death by trying to mount her own sting operation on the man she considered responsible. Not a real sensible response, but definitely not that of a fragile woman. Seth's chuckle was as much pained as amused. "I think she's got precious little in common with Tom's Allison."

"I think you're right," Raz said, and started for the door. "I guess we'd better show up for that breakfast the Valkyrie has waiting for us." At the door he added casually, "I wouldn't assume that, just because Tom's reasons for wanting Sophie are a little cloudy, he's going to step back. He's under the impression that all you want from her are a few tussles in bed."

Seth froze, unfamiliar anger clouding his brain. "He said that?"

"More or less."

It took a minute for Seth to remember what he'd told Tom. "Just because I'm not interested in marriage doesn't mean I'm only after fun and games."

"What are you after?" Fortunately, Raz didn't wait for an answer before he headed down the hall.

Seth followed more slowly.

Raz, damn him, had asked a good question. Just what did he want from Sophie? At the moment, he had no answer. But one thing was certain. He was not letting her out of the house today.

Nine

"Quit pouting," Sophie said. "I compromised, didn't I? And nothing happened."

Seth didn't answer as he turned down Sophie's wide, tree-lined street. He didn't think much of her idea of compromise. She'd flatly refused to stay put. She had cut down on her hours at the home, bringing some of the work back with her, and she'd agreed to let Seth drive her there and stay with her, but she wouldn't take any of North's men along. Since Sophie was paying for the guards, she was technically in charge of them.

His mistake, Seth acknowledged. He should have had North bill him, but he'd been trying to respect her sense of independence. At least they were nearly back to her house and, as she'd said, nothing had happened.

The children had surprised Seth. So had his reaction to them.

The home housed thirty kids of both sexes and all ages, and Sophie was obviously a favorite with them. Nothing surprising there, since she was just as obviously crazy about them. Quite a few had found reasons to go to Sophie's office. Maybe, like she'd said, they'd needed the reassurance of seeing her to know she was really all right after she'd disappeared for days.

The kids had stared at his scars. Seth had expected that and was braced for it. But none of them seemed frightened or repulsed by his appearance. When the smaller ones asked him what happened to his face, Seth said simply that he'd been burned. With all except a tiny charmer with red pigtails, that explanation was enough.

With the little redhead, though, his terse explanation didn't end her interest. She climbed up in Seth's lap and put both small, grubby hands on his face. He flinched when she rubbed the scarred side, prepared for the crushing onslaught of remembered failure. She was about the same size, the same age...

"Thorry," she said, and changed the rub to a powder-soft pat. "Doth your burn thtill hurt? It'th really big. Want to thee mine?" With all the dispatch and immodesty of a four-year-old, she squirmed around in his lap and pulled up her dress, and he saw.

Her burns were indeed a lot smaller—five round, angry scars along her upper thigh that looked damnably like cigarette burns, intentionally inflicted.

The sight of those hideously neat little burns somehow short-circuited Seth's downward spiral into guilt. He said something to her—he didn't know what—and after she left he looked at Sophie.

"Her mother," Sophie told him quietly, "doesn't have custody anymore. That's why she's here."

Seth slowed as he turned into Sophie's driveway so that North's man, the one situated at the front of the drive, could get a visual ID. It had rained while they were at the home, and the bright afternoon sunlight drew sparkles from the damp paving stones. "When we pulled up here yesterday," Sophie said, "I felt like I'd been gone for years, not days."

"How do you feel now?" He climbed out of the pickup and started around it, but she didn't wait on him before opening her door and getting out.

"Confused." She smiled, the most full, genuine smile he'd seen on her face since they left the mountain. "But I'm working on it. Getting out, seeing the children helped."

A car drove past. The *shush-shush* of tires on the wet road in front of the house reminded Seth of Sunday mornings and going to church, maybe because cars here moved so sedately along the wide roads. Maybe because this neighborhood seemed permanently dressed in its Sunday best.

When he heard one of those cars pull into the driveway he spun around, then relaxed as he recognized Tom's Jeep. Tom pulled up behind them and stopped.

Everything happened at once.

The front door of the house opened. Rocky shot out past the guard stationed by the door, barking happily and heading straight at them. Mrs Porter lumbered after the dog, yelling something. Tom opened the door of his Jeep and stepped out. Seth called Rocky, who ignored him, leaping full weight against Sophie and nearly knocking her down just as a car backfired twice.

Backfired?

"Get her down!" Tom yelled as the guard by the drive dropped into firing position, aimed at the street, and the cannon-boom of a .357 rattled windows for a block around.

Seth launched himself while Tom leapt back into the Jeep and jammed it into reverse. Rocky jumped and yelped happily around Sophie, who looked bewildered as she lifted her hand to her torn sleeve, to the streak of bright crimson on her arm.

Seth slammed into her as if she were the tackling dummy at high school practice. Her breath whooshed out. The paving stones scraped his side as he landed, his arms circling her. He rolled, covering her with his body. The guard from the door raced toward them.

On the quiet street, tires squealed as a car peeled out. Rocky planted her feet on Seth's back and tried to lick his face. Seth shoved the dog away and heard Tom's Jeep peel out.

For a minute he kept his head down. His heartbeat raced out of control, and his breath shuddered through him. Beneath him, Sophie was still, except for the rise and fall of her chest that told him she was alive. Alive.

He lifted his head and looked into wide green eyes more startled than scared.

"I love you," he said.

Then she looked frightened.

Six hours later, the bathroom was already steamy when Sophie opened the door of the oversize shower stall. She stepped under the stream of hot water, cupping the elbow of her hurt arm with her other hand to support it, and she shook. For a few minutes she gave in to the shakes, trying to think only of the heat, the soothing sensation of water running down her body.

She was not going to go to Seth.

The doctor at the emergency room had told her she was lucky, that the bullet had barely creased her upper arm. Tom had said she was lucky, because Tyburn Madison was apparently relying on his own personnel. A professional hit man wouldn't have missed the shot, even with Rocky's interference.

Sophie didn't feel lucky.

Her arm didn't hurt too badly anymore, though at the time she could have sworn it was sliced open to the bone. The wound had hurt like crazy and, according to worry-wart Seth, could have sent her into shock. Sophie had decided that Hollywood had misled the entire country about what was involved in "just a crease" from a rifle bullet.

Her shaking eased gradually. She'd done what she had to do after she came home from the hospital. She couldn't stand the idea of being hypnotized by someone she'd never met, so she'd contacted Dr. Tarnelli, a therapist she knew from her work at the home. Dr. Tarnelli used hypnosis sometimes to deal with repressed memories.

When Sophie explained her situation, the doctor had agreed to see her right away. Her appointment was for ten-thirty tomorrow morning. Tom would accompany her so he could question her while she was under hypnosis, since it was possible she wouldn't retain her memories once she awoke.

In spite of the heat and the steam, Sophie shivered. She wasn't going to think about hypnosis, the unremembered parts of her past, or her too-vivid memory of an assassin's bullet. She needed to relax before she could hope to get any sleep. She really needed some sleep.

She did not need to lie awake in her big bed and think about Seth and how he would be just down the hall with his big, warm body and his big, careful hands. She didn't need that at all. Sleep would be much better than lying awake wondering how he would look if she went to him. He'd be surprised, maybe shocked, considering how carefully she'd avoided him since they got back from the emergency room.

Would he smile and let the sun inside the house, though dark had fallen outside? Or would he be too tight with hunger to smile, tight the way she was tight, like a cord drawn taut and vibrating—like a gyroscope, spinning and spinning.

He'd said he loved her.

She turned into the water and let it beat down on her bent head, hugging her wounded arm, blind and breathless from the water streaming over her head and shoulders, and knew she wasn't going to sleep. All the hot water in the world couldn't make her sleep tonight. She was going to lie awake and hurt herself with thinking about him.

But she wouldn't go to him. He deserved so much better. That much discipline she had.

Seth thought she was disciplined because she was a runner. She grimaced. Seth saw more in her than was there. Carefully, moving her right arm in fractional amounts, she poured some gel into her palm and began to wash.

She ran because it was *attainable,* because it was easy, not because she possessed any great strength of will. Put one foot in front of the other and keep doing it, that was running. Nothing complicated, no decisions to make, little chance of messing up your life. A misstep meant a twisted ankle, your own ankle. You didn't hurt other people that way. Oh, yes, she liked running.

Shaving her legs wasn't too hard, but washing her hair nearly did her in. While scrubbing one-handed, she stepped in a spot of shampoo she'd spilled because she hadn't put the lid back on, since that took two hands. She started to slide. Instinctively, her right hand shot out, grabbing at the wall, and pain shot up and down her arm. She cried out.

She shut the water off and stepped from the shower. Tears stood in her eyes. She managed to dry off, but she couldn't rebandage her arm or dry her hair or get a towel wrapped around her properly. When she realized she hadn't brought her robe into the bathroom, she wanted to cry. She was naked and stupid and useless, and her arm hurt. She went to the bathroom door and opened it.

Seth stood next to her big, blue satin bed. Looking straight at her.

She slammed the door shut.

Three seconds later she heard his voice right on the other side of the door. "Sophie? Are you okay?"

She leaned against the door. "Go away." The damned tears started leaking out.

"No."

He did like that word. She sniffed. "You have to go away. I'm naked."

"I noticed."

He was amused. She was going to kill him, only she couldn't open the door.

"Look, I'll get you a robe or something. But I'm not leaving. You've taken your bandage off, and you're going to need help with that arm."

It was hopeless. Seth was in his caretaker mode, and a locked door wouldn't stop him. She told him where to find her robe, wiped her eyes, unlocked the door and tried to position a towel in front of her.

Only he didn't just hand her the thick terry cloth robe through the door. He came right into the bathroom with her and started fussing. She was an idiot—no, not that arm, put the other one through the sleeve. She couldn't put anything on her wound when it wasn't even bandaged, for God's sake—and he didn't care if she did have to drop the towel! It was her own fault for washing her hair, of all things, when she was hurt and had no business locking the door, and didn't she realize she could have lain on that bathroom floor, unconscious, for hours before he could get in?

"Huh," she said inelegantly, giving up and dropping the damned towel so she could put her good arm through the sleeve he held for her. "Hours? You could *nag* it open in fifteen minutes or less."

He ignored her comment. "I can't believe you washed your hair." He passed the robe carefully under her hurt arm and brought it around front. "I would have done it if you'd asked. Or you could have paid someone to come here. Hell, you could have bought a damned salon if you wanted."

"Why were you lurking in my room, anyway?"

"I brought you a supper tray. I figured you were going to try and get away with skipping supper. Not a good idea." He finished bundling her up to his satisfaction and looked, for the first time, directly into her eyes. His hand lingered at her waist, where he'd tied the belt to hold the robe awkwardly in place. His hair hung loose, as dark and free as the eyes that met hers. And her heart stopped, then started, jumping like a jackrabbit fleeing from a coyote.

Because his nagging voice and solicitous hands had lied. He wasn't feeling . . . conscientious. Or nurselike. Or. . .

"We need to get your arm bandaged," he said softly, his dark eyes promising heat. Promising touches with his big, tender hands that wouldn't be quite so . . . careful. Speaking so plainly of pleasure and possession that what his mouth said made no sense. Or too much sense. "Come sit down, and I'll take care of you."

And she went with him, weak and quiet and pliable, self-ish with hope, when he took her arm and led her into her bedroom.

The air was cooler there, cool enough to raise chill bumps along her damp skin as he steered her to the bed and they sat, side by side. Cool enough to almost bring her out of the spelled daze his hot eyes had cast her into. "I can bandage it," she told him. "I took the old bandage off. If you'll give me the gauze, I can do it."

"Now, how could you?" He sounded so normal as he looked down at the supplies he'd brought in with them, his hair hiding his face, and she thought she was going crazy. She'd just imagined the look in his eyes because she wanted him, wanted him, wanted him . . .

"If the wound was on the lower part of your arm," he said as he tore open the large gauze pad, "you might man-age, but not with it so close to the shoulder." He looked up again.

He knew. Knew what he was doing to her and he meant to do it, liked unnerving her this way and intended to do other things to her, too, she saw in the promises tucked away in the secret darkness of his eyes. Her lips parted to let her shallow breaths out more easily.

His fingers were gentle. She knew that already, didn't she? And his gentle fingers did nothing suggestive as they ban-daged her arm. They stayed strictly to their business. Care-ful, caring fingers that would take no chances with her wound—careful, caring man who wanted her, and she knew she would give him anything, anything at all that he asked.

She throbbed and ached and cherished each gentle brush of his tending and knew she was going to give him herself, knowing who that self was this time, knowing how greedy and selfish she was to offer him so little when he came to her full of so much, and she would do it anyway if he wanted. If he wanted—

"There," he said softly as he smoothed the tape down. His fingers paused on her arm as he looked into her eyes. "Does it hurt very much, Sophie?"

Did it? She had no idea. She shook her head.

"That's good," he whispered.

His fingers slid up her bare shoulder to her neck and lingered under her jaw, stroking lightly. The storm in his eyes came closer. So did his mouth, so close she could no longer see his lips as they whispered along her jaw—could only feel the hot, moist air of his words.

"Do you want me, Sophie?"

"You—" She quivered all over when his lips skimmed her cheek. "You know this is wrong."

"Why?" His mouth glanced off of her lips once and hovered over her eyelids while his hand went to her waist. He began untying the belt he'd so carefully fastened a few minutes ago.

"I'm not what you need," she said desperately as her robe fell open, one side puddling in her lap.

"Why?" He drew the other side of the robe off her shoulder then paused, looking at her breasts. Briefly his knuckles turned white where he gripped the soft terry cloth, white with the lightning that flashed in his eyes. But when he looked up, a smile touched his mouth. "Because you can't return my feelings?"

Why couldn't she be stronger? Strong enough to do something other than moan his name?

His hands rose to her breasts. Cupped them. "Is this just sex for you, then, Sophie?" The thumbs of those big hands easily reached her nipples, and he rubbed her. The lightning struck, arching her back in a delicious spasm. He bent to nibble at her mouth, and his hands kneaded her thankful breasts, building and assuaging the ache, while he teased her lips with his.

"This *is* just sex, isn't it?" he murmured into the warm cavern of her mouth when she opened it, begging him to come in. But he pulled back, bent and pressed a kiss to the upper curve of her breast. "Isn't it?"

"Yes," she whispered as she grabbed his head and pulled it to her, putting a stop to the torment and getting his mouth where she needed it. "Yes," she said again as his lips fastened on her nipple and pulled, as he licked, then sucked.

And "yes" she said over and over, along with less coherent urgings as they took her robe off and removed some of his clothes but not all, because he'd made her crazy with wanting and needing and she couldn't wait. And maybe he was a little crazy with wanting, too. He moaned as he sank into her, into the part of her that hurt and wept for him. Then he began to move, and the gyroscope spun out of control.

The lights were off, the covers were off, and the woman sprawled across Seth was bonelessly, thoroughly, happily sated. "You're a monster," she told his chest, her lips barely moving.

"Mmm," he said, having no breath for anything more. He'd made sure, when they collapsed after the last loving, that her arm rested comfortably where it wouldn't be jostled. Then he'd rested his hand on her head, thinking of stroking her hair. But he hadn't the energy to do it.

"A terrible, ravenous beast," she said, adding smugly, "You've ruined me with your demands. Three times, Seth. That's excessive, isn't it? Three times."

Yes, it had been three, hadn't it? "Mmm," he said again, and if the smile he smiled into the darkness was a trifle smug as well, no one could see.

"Your hand is heavy," she said. "Your fingers are in my face."

"I'm sorry," he said. "Something terrible has happened to my body. This voracious witch jumped my bones and drained my life force. I may never move again."

He felt the shape of her smile in the way her cheek bunched beneath his fingers. They lay together, silent and sated in the darkness. He didn't say that he loved her, though the feeling swelled in him, a rolling wave like those in midocean, smooth and complete without the shore to break itself upon.

Soon he felt more than heard the sinking steadiness of her breath that told him she was drifting into sleep. He was glad. Sleep would ease the strain he'd seen around her eyes, probably more thoroughly than he'd done with the wild loving he'd given—and taken from—her.

Surely he shouldn't have. Surely he should have held off, at least until her arm healed. Surely, loving her like he did, he could have waited to claim her again until she was more whole and certain in her life. Until no one was trying to kill her.

But when he was losing himself in her and aware, so aware, that he could make her lose herself, too—when he buried himself deeply in the giving heat of her body and nothing, nothing at all lay between them, then he could believe she loved him. He could convince himself he saw it in her eyes, heard it in the low, desperate sounds she made, felt it when she dug her fingers into his flesh as she pulled him farther into her.

In the middle of loving he was certain of her. Certain she *did* love him, whether she admitted it or not. Somehow, someway, his valiant Sophie had become convinced of her unworthiness. Somehow a woman who could take on a major drug dealer, who could escape a killer while blood ran down her face and cross the slope of a storm-wrecked mountain at midnight, didn't think she possessed any strength or courage.

He lay there in the darkness, chewing on his doubts until he realized she must be cold. He had the warm little furnace of her body covering him, but she had no covers at all. Very gently, he moved her onto her back. She murmured something and slept on. He had to get out of bed to retrieve their covers—they'd been rather athletic with their second coupling, after refueling on the supper he'd brought her. When he climbed back into her bed, pulling her cotton sheet and satin comforter up over them both, she cuddled into him as naturally as a puppy.

Then he lay quietly in Sophie's bed and tried not to ask himself what he would do if she did love him.

She was rich. Tom had asked if her money was a problem for him, and now that Seth was no longer fooling himself about loving her, he wondered. He had money himself. Not as much as she did, but enough, enough for him, at any rate. Sophie seemed completely unimpressed by her own wealth, but hadn't he thought Linda was different from the others in her milieu? He'd been as wrong as a man could be about Linda...and yet, as he breathed in Sophie's scent and cherished the weight of her limp, warm body snuggled up against him, he knew she was nothing like his former fiancée.

No, Sophie's money wouldn't be the problem. He would be.

This house had been in her family for generations. It was her one surviving link with that family. How could he ask her to give it up, to live with him on his mountain, where they couldn't even be sure of having electricity all the time? He couldn't imagine her giving up her contact with the kids at the home, either. But he couldn't live in Houston again. The surgeon had done wonders with his knee and the splintered bone of his calf, but that leg would never be wholly dependable. When Seth had realized he'd never fight fires again, he'd known he had to get out of Houston.

For some reason he thought of the little red-haired girl at the children's home, whose burns "didn't hurt anymore." She'd shown him the scars, though. Didn't that mean the burns hadn't really stopped hurting, that the damage went too deep, and she had to make sure everyone saw her scars, and knew? Or was the little four-year-old girl stronger, wiser, more resilient than Seth, and able to let the pain go?

Was it ever possible to just let go?

The issue of where he and Sophie could be together might not arise. Someone was trying to kill her. Someone she couldn't remember, who might succeed, unthinkable as it was, if the people guarding Sophie made any mistakes. Seth lay cold and awake long into the night, in spite of the warmth of the woman beside him and the weight of the covers, and knew how wrong Sophie was about him.

He could fail. He had before. This time, if he made a mistake Sophie would be the one to pay for his failure—with her life.

Ten

———

The dream drove Seth from Sophie's bed early the next morning.

He leaned forward, into the window. Slowly, agonizingly slowly. It was like pushing against time, against the invisible wall of fate . Then he saw the faces...

He awoke weak and sweating in the predawn gray. He should have known the dream would come. Last night he'd lain awake trying to think of ways to keep Sophie's enemy from hurting her. Then he'd fallen asleep and dreamed.

Two girls. One, barely into her teens, with terrified eyes and dark hair. One younger, very young, in a white and pink nightgown.

The driving spray of the shower in her bathroom helped. He'd learned ways of coping with the dream, and water was good for driving away the stink it left behind. He stood under the shower for a long time.

When he got out he wrapped a towel around his waist, then found Sophie's razor and a fresh blade. The mirror above her vanity was fogged over, and he was glad. Every day of his life he shaved, and that intimate connection with the changed terrain of his face was enough. He didn't need to confront his reflection over and over.

A pink can held shaving gel with a prissy, feminine smell. He lathered his face and was about to start shaving when the bathroom door opened.

"Hi, there," Sophie said, and smiled.

She wore his shirt, just like she had at the cabin. The sight of her fresh from sleep, her eyes still muzzy with dreams, hit him with the forceful inevitability of the ocean breaking against the shore, crashing over swimmers and surfers, rocks and shells and sand. The conviction of his own uselessness was a merciless undertow pulling him down, down.

The littlest girl screamed.

How could he keep Sophie safe?

Seth didn't speak. He couldn't. He faced the fogged-over mirror and drew the razor along the bumpy skin of his jaw.

He always shaved the left side of his face first. It was the trickiest. Some of the skin had been grafted from his thighs, so it grew a few silly, straggly hairs. He probably could have skipped this part of his face—who would notice a few hairs in the midst of this ruin?—but he never did. Shaving connected him to the man he used to be.

It linked him to someone else, too—the person on whose behalf he kept his scars.

"There, sweetheart," he crooned. *"I'm just a man under all this stuff. Not a beast or a monster..."*

He felt cooler air on his legs and chest and realized Sophie had left the bathroom door open. He glanced at the mirror. The fog was clearing up rapidly. "Do you have to stare?" he asked, turning slightly so he didn't see the mirror. "Haven't you ever seen a man shave?"

"Sorry." But she didn't look away. She moved closer. "Seth, I've been thinking about this hypnosis thing..."

...he felt her slight weight in his arms. Then the hell-wall exploded, and he threw himself back, back, off the ladder

*but he couldn't fall, his legs were locked and so one of them
snapped like a dry twig as his weight carried him back. His
mouth froze open in a rictus of pain while hell feasted on his
face and on the small, living burden in his arms and
screamed silently in the thin, high breeze that held the
sweetish stink of burned flesh—*

"God," he said, leaning against the sink, hating himself.
Hating her for being there, for bringing the dream back,
seeing him like this. "For God's sake, Sophie, you aren't
trying to back out of the hypnosis, are you?"

"I don't like the idea," she said. "And what will it help
if I do remember? There has to be some other way to—Seth?
Are you okay?" She touched his arm.

He jerked as if her hand were a lash striking him. "Some
other way? Grow up, Sophie. There's damn little anyone can
do to protect you if you're not willing to do anything for
yourself."

He didn't look at her. The foam on his unshaven cheek
itched as it dried. He registered that tiny discomfort, along
with the rackety beat of his heart, in the long pause that
followed.

"Something *is* wrong," she said, and the tremor in her
voice made him hate himself even more. "Talk to me, Seth.
This has to do with your burns, doesn't it?" She reached out
again, touching his shoulder next to the scar tissue.

Her hands had been all over him last night. All over. Delicious, hot little hands that he'd craved and delighted in.
This morning, feeling her fingers on his damaged skin made
him nauseous. This time, he felt that she was touching him
while the wounds were still open. "I can't talk about it." He
turned away from her and faced the mirror, where he met his
own eyes, trapped in the face of the Beast.

"We're going to have to talk about it sometime, Seth."

He managed to break away from the mirror's taunting
reflection. "Do you really expect me to confide in a 'poor
little rich girl' who runs away and hides whenever life gets
unpleasant?"

He might as well have hit her. The blood left her face, then flooded back in two livid patches on her cheeks. "I've never heard you lie before." She turned and left without closing the door.

Seth stood without moving for a long time, his hands clenched into fists at his sides. The dried foam on his face itched. Behind him, water still ran from the faucet and splashed in the sink. Seth turned, cupped his hands beneath the running water and rinsed his face.

He wished he could hide, he thought viciously, lifting his head. But his fingers on the rough surface of his cheek told him the truth: he was changed. Damaged. Forever, irreparably altered, and there was no going back. And memory, for him, wasn't the hide-and-seek partner it seemed to be for Sophie. Memory was inexorably real, a visitor that came, not so often these days, but still it came and sat with him for a time, making itself more vivid than the present.

His reflection stared back at him, clear as glass in the unfogged mirror—and still, after two years, he recognized only half of his face, the smooth, human half—still the other half looked like a monster from a nightmare, not like him. Not him.

Except that it was him, wasn't it?

And I, he thought slowly, *had the nerve to accuse* her *of hiding.*

Sophie showered and dressed in one of the guest bedrooms. Her arm was stiff and sore, but it moved more easily today, which was just as well, because she'd forgotten the sling when she pulled her things hastily from drawers and the closet and fled her room.

She grimaced when she saw what she'd grabbed to wear. The dress was a long, barely opaque drift of white designed to be worn over a matching petticoat, made decent on top only by the abundance of white embroidery on the sheer vest. White on white seemed singularly inappropriate after the night she'd just passed.

But she wasn't going back to her room to change. Not because she was avoiding Seth, either. She wasn't going to give in to the urge to hide herself away there.

So the next hour Sophie didn't hide. She played with Rocky and petted the puppies until Mrs. Porter started growling about dogs and people being underfoot. Then she took her breakfast outside and drank her juice, ignored the eggs, and fed most of the toast to the sparrows. When the clouds overhead threatened a drenching she went back inside and made some necessary phone calls. The press had found out about the shooting yesterday, and she didn't want her friends to worry. She avoided the avalanche of incoming calls from acquaintances and the avid press, thanking God for the dour bulk of Mrs. Porter placed solidly between her and an intrusive world.

But at least, she thought, curled up in the reading room in the square of weak sunshine that framed her father's chair, she hadn't hidden away in her room again. She had stayed in obvious parts of the house, where Seth could have found her if he'd wanted to.

Apparently he hadn't.

In her lap lay the first volume of Tolkien's trilogy. She'd gotten to page ten before she quit pretending she was reading. Over and over in her mind she played out what Seth had said. What she had said. What she should have said and done differently.

She'd handled it all wrong. She wasn't used to being brave. Speaking up about Seth's wounds while the darkness sat on his face and his pain rose from him in waves was about as brave as she'd ever been. But what business did she have inviting him to confide in her? Implying that he could count on her, when her own experience said he couldn't?

The door opened. Seth stood there in his worn jeans, with his dark hair tied back and his expression as set and implacable as the rock that made up his mountain. The restlessness that had plagued her all morning surged, sending her to her feet. Her book fell to the floor.

He came in quietly, moving with the grace she'd noticed from the first, and closed the door behind him. He wasn't limping much. She was glad he hadn't strained his bad leg yesterday when he tackled her and protected her body with his own.

He stopped several steps away from her. "I'm sorry."

All of a sudden, with him standing grimly expressionless in front of her, she was angry. "You had no business saying that to me."

"No, I didn't."

"Saying you're sorry doesn't make it go away. And you were wrong. Maybe I have hidden from problems in the past, but I'm changing." Anger felt good. Heady. Free. She stepped toward him, furious that she'd spent the past two hours telling herself she deserved his rejection. "And maybe I don't understand exactly what you went through, but I could listen if you'd ever open up and talk to me. I don't have to stick my head in a fire to know it hurts, and I don't have to apologize for having an undamaged body just because you don't!"

She knew, in the abrupt silence that followed her words, in the sudden pallor around his eyes, that she'd hurt him. "Oh, God." She stepped toward him. "I'm sorry. I didn't mean—"

The knock that landed on the door startled her. Mrs. Porter had the door open before Sophie even got her mouth closed around the rest of her plea.

"It's that other policeman," the housekeeper said with distaste. "He says he's here to drive you to your appointment."

Dr. Tarnelli's tiny reception area was austere. The walls were done in alternating peach and rust, with white woodwork and white-on-white pressed paper pictures. Two bare Shaker-style tables separated the four plain chairs.

Sophie didn't like it.

"You said she told you ten-thirty," Seth muttered, frowning at the closed door that led, presumably, to the doctor's office. He and Sophie were alone in the reception room. Dr. Tarnelli didn't employ a receptionist, and Tom had dropped them off, then gone to park the car. "It's ten thirty-five."

"Is it?" She uncrossed her legs and then crossed them the other way, unable to sit still. "We can't start until your cousin gets here, anyway. He wants to listen in."

Seth glanced at her. His face softened. "It won't be so bad," he told her. "You said you know this woman and like her. Remember?"

"Yes, but—" She gave up and stood. "Oh, it's ridiculous to be this jittery." This scared.

"Not ridiculous. Uncomfortable, maybe." He stood, too.

Their eyes met. They'd had no time or privacy to talk. The unresolved feelings from their argument simmered behind Seth's eyes.

"What if I can't remember?" she whispered. "What if I remember but it doesn't help?" *What if remembering makes me lose you?*

The door to the hall swung open and Tom came in, pulling off his Stetson and overcrowding the small room. He slapped his hat against his leg, sending water droplets flying. "Sorry," he said. "The rain's making a mess of visibility, so I had one of North's men come inside to keep an eye on the main entrance. The other man is watching the rear exit from his car. Hope I haven't kept everyone waiting."

"It's a wonder you didn't rent an armored car and put me in it," Sophie muttered. The elaborate precautions Seth and Tom had insisted on for her to undertake a simple drive to the doctor's office made her jitters a good deal worse.

"Ms. Cochran?" said a pleasant female voice.

Sophie turned to the woman who'd just opened her office door. "Yes?"

"I'm Rachel Tarnelli." Dr. Tarnelli was a short, fiftyish black woman with the trace of an Italian accent. The doctor glanced at the two large men filling up her reception room. "I suppose one of you gentlemen is the detective? I understand why you must be present during the session, but I'll need to explain a few things before we begin."

Seth and Tom each stepped forward, offering their names and a handshake. The doctor explained that Sophie wouldn't "hear" anyone but her during the session, so Tom's questions would have to be channeled through her. "If you'll step inside, Detective," Dr. Tarnelli said when Tom agreed to her terms, "I'll show you where I'd like you to sit. Are you ready, Ms. Cochran?"

Sophie stood. She took one step toward the doctor, then stopped.

She didn't want Seth to go in with her. She didn't want him to hear the things she would learn about herself in that office. She didn't know where she found the courage to speak. "Doctor," she said quietly, "I'd like both men to be present."

Dr. Tarnelli's inner office was nothing like the reception area. Decorative debris from several countries sat on the shelves, her desk, and the floor in a colorful jumble. The only similarity between the two spaces was the clean, functional lines of the Shaker furniture. In that personal, cluttered space, Sophie felt a little more comfortable.

Dr. Tarnelli directed Seth and Tom to a small love seat that immediately looked much smaller with the two men crowding it. Sophie was invited to sit in one of the two chairs across from the desk. The doctor sat in the other chair. "Pull your chair around to face me," she said briskly, "and we'll talk."

They talked about Sophie's job at the home. They talked about why Sophie was in danger, what led up to it and what she did remember, and gradually Sophie was talking less and listening more. It was really very comfortable in the cozy, colorful office, and Dr. Tarnelli easy to listen to... not that Sophie felt the slightest bit hypnotized, but she didn't mind following the woman's suggestion to imagine herself in a pleasant, restful place. Like the cabin, Sophie thought... a place where nothing could harm her, where she could be very still, very peaceful...

...so when Charles told you he was leaving the party early, you knew he would be away from his apartment for some time. What did you do after he left? You went to your car? Why?

"I'd left an old pair of running shoes in the trunk. I didn't want to sneak around in high heels, so I put them on."

Then what did you do?

"I drove to Charles's apartment." It was funny. Most of Sophie was in her car, coping with an incredible attack of nerves now that she was finally putting her plan into action. But she could hear the woman's voice perfectly well, and her own voice, too—though sometimes she wasn't sure if she was talking or thinking—and another voice sometimes. A man's voice. But the woman had told her she wouldn't understand what the man said, and the woman was right. The man's voice rumbled something, but it didn't make any sense. And then the woman spoke again.

How are you going to get into Charles's apartment while he's gone, Sophie? Do you have a key?

Christine's key. She had her sister's key, one she'd found in Christine's things last month, and she'd already checked it visually against the key she'd seen Charles use. It should work. It should—yes, the door swung open soundlessly.

The apartment was very dark. Sophie felt almost sick with fear, her heart pounding, her mouth so dry the air burned when she breathed it in. But she went in. For Christine. She closed the door and fumbled for the light switch with her right hand, the one that wasn't carrying the tote.

What tote is that, Sophie?

"The one from the trunk of my car. The one with the bags of white powder."

Sophie heard the man's voice in the background again, but it wasn't important. What mattered was that this was her chance. She had to get over this terror and do what she came here for.

What did you say, Sophie?

"This is my chance." She knew she couldn't really make it up to Christine. Her sister was dead. It was forever too late to have another chance with Christine. "If we'd been close the way sisters should be, she would have listened when I told her about Charles. So this is all I can do for her. I can make sure he doesn't hurt any more young girls."

How will you do that?

"I'll change his bags of powder for mine. I hope I used the right baggies, the same kind *they* use. Leila wasn't sure. She told me they use the little plastic bags you get at the grocery store, but she wasn't sure which brand." And that was a year ago. They might have changed.

Who's Leila?

"She's the one Charles seduced last year. I asked around until I found out what happened to her, where she'd gone. Her parents put her in a drug rehabilitation center in another city. I went and talked to her."

Leila had wanted to stop Charles, too. The plan, in fact, was hers, and most of the details on how to make the substitution, because Sophie knew nothing about drugs, while the damaged young woman still in her teens knew all too much. But now that Sophie was here, actually here in Charles's apartment with a tote full of little sacks of white flour, the plan seemed stupid, incredibly stupid. And wrong.

What's wrong?

"It's wrong, and I don't know if I can—oh, no! I tripped over something and spilled the tote." She got down on her hands and knees and started shoving the baggies back into the tote. Thank God none of them had come open. That would be all she needed, she thought, fighting back a hysterical laugh. To spill flour on Charles's immaculate blue carpet and have to hunt up his vacuum in the middle of the night while breaking in to plant phony drugs on him.

Why did you bring plastic bags of flour to Charles's apartment, Sophie?

"I have to find the supply. Leila told me where he kept it. If he hasn't changed hiding places, I'll swap some of my baggies for some of his, then I'll flush the contents from his baggies down the toilet. Then *they* will stop him. The police can't, but the people he works for—if they think he's tricking them, they'll—" But she didn't know if she could go through with it. She zipped up the tote again, but her hands shook. She spotted a baggie that she'd missed, grabbed it and stuck it in her pocket.

A man's voice intruded, tugging at her, and for a moment she felt a hard wooden chair beneath her bottom and thought she heard another voice, another man talking, but—

Is that what you do, Sophie? Do you exchange the bags?

She found the stash. It was just where Leila had said it would be. Stupid Charles, think up one trick and keep playing it over and over. She stared at the cardboard box full of tidy little bags of cocaine that looked just like her own neatly filled bags, only these were so deadly.

And she couldn't do it. God, she'd been crazy to come here. She felt as if she'd suddenly woken from an awful dream to find herself kneeling on the floor of Charles's bedroom in front of his closet, staring at two dozen bags of cocaine.

How could she have thought she could do this, could arrange the death of another person? Because that's what she'd be doing—as surely as if she held the gun, she'd be setting Charles Farquhar up to be killed.

She started to scramble to her feet, wanting nothing but to be gone, out of there long before Charles came home, when pain exploded in her head.

Nausea. She was going to be sick, she was throwing up—

Rain slashing her face, blood in her eyes and running, running—

Charles. She saw him standing in front of a huge stone fireplace, saw his face clearly in the soft, well-bred lighting of a private home—his handsome face slack and stupid with fear. The white stone gargoyles on the fireplace spoke in a man's voice, and her head hurt and hurt . . .

A car. Facedown in the back seat and she couldn't breath right and she slid, almost falling from the seat as the car slid. She half woke from a stupor and sick, she was going to be sick again—rain slashing her face, a woman's voice telling her it was all right—it wasn't all right—a gunshot and running and terror so huge it ate her and she was kneeling on the floor of Charles's bedroom when her head exploded and the lightning burst in front of her and a man, there was a huge man in the center of the storm with dark hair the wind loved and a ruined face and she ran to him and—

Come back, come all the way back now, to this room, to the present moment, and relax. Everything is all right now. What you remember is in the past. You're not there anymore, and you're safe . . .

"Here you go, honey," the woman's soft voice said. Sophie felt a light touch at the back of her head. "Here's that drink you wanted."

Sophie shuddered and took the glass in two shaky hands. Dr. Tarnelli bent over her, resting her hand on Sophie's shoulder. Her quick, black eyes flicked to the side. "Sit *down*, Mr. Brogan."

"I'm all right," Sophie said. Though it was obvious, from the weakness in her voice, that she wasn't. She sipped the water and tried to get her shakes under control. The doctor stayed at her side, patting her shoulder. Sophie didn't have to look behind her to feel Seth's impatience, his desire to come to her, comfort her.

Thank God Dr. Tarnelli wouldn't let him. What Sophie had to do would be difficult enough. She couldn't afford to give in to her need for him.

After a moment the doctor sat down again in her straight-backed chair. Sophie took a slow, careful breath. Not enough. She didn't remember enough, or maybe she remembered too much. Enough to damn her. Not enough to save her.

She didn't remember seeing who had ordered Charles Farquhar and herself killed. She did remember planning to set him up to be killed.

God. She thought she was going to throw up.

She looked at the woman facing her. "I'm never going to remember any more than I did today, am I?"

"Probably not." Dr. Tarnelli's gaze slipped to the men behind Sophie for a moment, then returned. "In my opinion, the patchy condition of your memory surrounding the moment you received the blow to your head is due to physiological, rather than psychological, causes. In other words, the damage is physical. It's unlikely you will ever recall more of that night than you do right now."

Hope was slow and stubborn to die, in spite of what Sophie herself felt to be true. "But I *might* remember the rest of it? I've been remembering more, in chunks, ever since I woke up..." At Seth's cabin. The place she'd used as a symbol of peace and safety, a place she would never see again.

The woman's face gentled even more. "I think, from what you and the others have told me, that your condition right after your injury was a combination of physical trauma, which caused your initial confusion, followed by a period of denial. You gave yourself time to get a little distance between you and events that were extremely painful. The reasons for that memory 'loss,' and this one, are quite different."

When Tom asked the doctor a question, Sophie's attention turned inward. She didn't want to think about the two men who'd been in the room while she recaptured all she'd ever know of a night that happened two lifetimes and ten days ago.

Only ten days... behind her sat the two men she didn't want to think about. One man, the policeman, was no doubt disappointed she would be of so little help in his investigation. The other man...

Used to love me, Sophie thought, squeezing her eyes closed. Because he couldn't, not anymore, not knowing what they both knew about her now. She couldn't let him.

Sophie sat very straight in the hard-backed chair and tried to live with that thought. She kept her eyes closed while the doctor told the two men to wait in the reception area for a few minutes so she could speak with her client privately. Sophie heard the office door open, then close. And from within the dark, acid-washed space behind her closed eyes, she said goodbye to Seth.

Although, knowing Seth, she thought wearily as she opened her eyes again, it wouldn't be that simple.

Seth stood in the little reception area with his back to the closed office door. "Put the word out. You can do that. Leak what you learned in this session so the bastard will know she isn't a threat to him."

"Madison isn't going to believe it," Tom said. "He can't afford to. She was hit over the head, taken to his house, and probably heard him give the order for both her and Farquhar to be killed. He won't believe she doesn't remember."

Seth's leg ached. His muscles had been tensed too long, the whole time he'd sat in there, forcing himself not to move, not to interfere, while Sophie traveled backward into hell. "You're sure it was Madison's house she was taken to?" he asked abruptly. "She doesn't remember seeing him."

"She saw the fireplace. That damned stone fireplace he has in his den, with the gargoyles flanking the mantel, is unique."

"Pretty stupid of him to have her brought to his home."

"Contrary to popular impression, most criminals aren't all that smart," Tom said dryly. "Madison himself is sly as a fox, but not all the people working for him are equally bright. The department has reason to believe Madison intended to kill Farquhar when he summoned him from that party. The man had become a liability, with his habit of seducing young women from good families and turning them into druggies. I figure Madison sent a man to retrieve Farquhar's supply from his apartment. His man found Sophie there and, not being one of the bright ones, he knocked her out and brought her back with him."

And Sophie had, apparently, come around while at Madison's house long enough to register that image of Farquhar standing in front of the fireplace. She might have seemed conscious to the others in the room, even responded to questions, without being fully aware. Without ever being able to remember it, because her brain simply hadn't recorded those moments.

"How do you suppose she got away?" Tom asked.

"The storm." Absently Seth rubbed the tired muscles above his knee. "We can't be sure, but she described sliding around in the back seat as if the car stopped suddenly, or slid out of control. They must have dumped her back there without tying her. I didn't see any rope marks on her, remember. She was unconscious, and female, and they underestimated her." *Like she underestimates herself.*

"It makes sense," Tom said. "The car runs into something, or stops suddenly to avoid hitting a deer or a downed tree. Maybe the driver and guard are stunned briefly. Sophie gets out and starts running. They don't go after her, or can't find her because of the storm. They've still got Farquhar in the car to deal with, so they give up on her for the time being and take Farquhar to the spot they've picked out, nice and remote. They shoot him and leave his body for the scavengers.'' Tom nodded. ''If that ranger hadn't been out looking for a missing hiker, who knows how long it would have been before Farquhar's body was found?''

Everything was making sense, Seth thought, from the running shoes she'd worn with her evening clothes to the plastic bag—that damned, damning bag of white powder he'd found in her pocket. And the contents had been innocent after all. Flour. After all his doubting and hers, the bag only held flour. But its purpose hadn't been so innocent, and now they both knew why seeing that bag had filled her with guilt.

One thing didn't make sense—the deep foreboding that filled Seth and had nothing to do with the ongoing threat of Tyburn Madison. The terrible sense Seth had that somehow, in learning Sophie's secrets, he'd lost her. She hadn't looked at him. Not once since she woke from her tranced state had she looked—

The office door opened. Sophie came out, a pale wraith in her white filmy dress and vest, her face almost as colorless as when Seth had first laid her, unconscious and bleeding, in his bed. She looked straight at Seth. ''We need to talk.''

Eleven

Sophie didn't deny herself the comfort of Seth's hand on her arm as they left Dr. Tarnelli's office. Maybe she was too selfish to give up that last touch. Maybe she just didn't want to hurt him any more than she already had...because she could see by the bleak determination on his face that he suspected her purpose, and that it hurt.

Tom stayed behind to use the doctor's phone. He would call the security men who'd been watching the building. Sophie couldn't leave without getting his all-clear.

In silence, Seth and Sophie walked down the short hall to the atrium at the center of the building. The black, fecund earth in the circular bed, the lush growth of the plants, the stink of recently applied fertilizer—all combined in a way that struck her as vaguely obscene. Overhead, rain beat a hushed tattoo on the skylight.

"Seth," she began, forcing herself to face him. To face what she was doing.

"No. I'm not going to let you say it." His big palms covered her shoulders. "Sophie, give yourself time to adjust to what you remembered today. Don't leap off a bridge because you're upset."

She turned away. In spite of her resolve, she couldn't look at him and do this. Several yards away, at the glass doors, she saw North's man watching the traffic outside. "So," she said, her voice wavering, "you'd compare breaking off with you to leaping off a bridge?"

He didn't answer. Not with words. He pulled her quickly, firmly to him, and he kissed her, and she—in spite of everything she knew she must do—was weak and stupid. She went lax and yearning against him, her hands limp against his chest, her belly cradling his sex, her mouth open and everything—her mouth, belly, everything—was his.

Tears stood in her eyes when he pulled back and looked down at her.

"Oh, hell," he said. He ran his knuckle under each of her eyes, skimming the moisture away. "Don't cry. Please don't."

She breathed in, trying for control. "I'm a coward. I run away from everything, and when I don't—when I try to face unpleasantness—I make everything worse." Her hands clenched into fists. "I was going to kill a man."

"No! There's a big difference between—"

"Between setting him up to be killed and doing it myself? The only difference I see is the kind of risk involved! I didn't want to risk being 'bad,' being caught and punished, so I found a way to get someone else to be responsible."

"And then couldn't do it. In the end, you couldn't do it." His thumb passed back and forth along her collarbone, a soothing, strumming motion. "Why do you remember everything else, and forget that? You are so very hard on yourself. I wish I could make you see what I see when I look at you."

"A poor little rich girl?" she said with involuntary, remembered hurt.

"You called me a liar then," he said quietly, "and you were right. You were right about something else, too. I was hiding from something ugly about myself. Not," he said with brief, bitter humor, "my face, for once." His eyelids lowered, as if he were still instinctively trying to hide. "I resented your wholeness. You saw that, or sensed it. That's why I was vicious to you. Because your body is perfect and beautiful, and mine isn't."

Something moved inside her, soul deep and painful. "Seth." She touched his cheek, searching for words, the right words, the ones that would make him stop hurting.

"Let me get this said." When his hand urged her to rest her head on his shoulder, she gave him that. His hand lingered at the nape of her neck, lightly rubbing. "I've hidden away in my cabin for the last two years and told myself it was because the sight of me troubled people. Sometimes I even believed that, as if I were being noble by taking myself out of the public eye. Mostly I knew I was selfish and cowardly. But I thought I just didn't want to see their reactions. The shocked fascination, or the averted eyes. It's like with the mirrors."

She wrapped her arms around his waist. *Later,* she told herself. Later she would make him see reason about her, about them. Not now.

He laid his head on the top of hers. "I hid from seeing people," he said softly. "Not from being seen. Everyone else was whole, and a part of me hated that."

She was not crying. She was *not.*

"You asked me about my injuries. Do you really want to know?"

"Tell me," she said, because whether she wanted to know or not, he needed to tell her.

"It was a fairly ordinary residential fire," he said, staring over her shoulder. "Unfortunately, the house was set back on a large, wooded plot. By the time a neighbor saw the fire and called it in, the fire was well advanced. The parents weren't at home, you see."

She went stiff in his arms. He didn't notice, continuing in a monotone. "The fire had started in the kitchen, just below the little girl's bedroom. There were two girls," he said. "One was thirteen. The other was four. Only four. We couldn't get upstairs from inside the house, which meant it had to be a ladder rescue. I went up. Hobbs was behind me. Procedure called for me to climb in the window, get the girls and pass the older one to Hobbs, then take the little one down myself. But there wasn't time. I knew it, could feel that we were out of time. You get to where you can read a fire. Not perfectly, but you get a feel for it. I was afraid the floor would pancake, or the oxygen from the window would turn smoldering materials into a blaze. So I leaned in the window and reached for the little girl. I was going to pass her to Hobbs, then take the older one." He fell silent.

She raised her head, but she couldn't see. Tears made prisms of the light from the skylight overhead. "Seth?"

"She was already terrified, and the sight of me in all my gear, the breathing mask and everything, panicked her. I pushed my mask off. Her sister put her in my arms and then—then the smoke exploded into flames. Flashover." He swallowed. "She burned in my arms, Sophie. I had on all the protective gear, and she had on a white nightgown with little pink flowers. She breathed in some of the flame, and she died."

Sophie's cheeks were wet. She didn't want to ask. She didn't. "Her sister? The older girl?"

"I hung there on the ladder. I couldn't move. I was still holding the little girl—I didn't know she was dead—and my calf and knee were broken. My face . . . burns hurt, Sophie. Such a small part of me was burned compared to what happened to her and her sister, but the pain was incredible. Later, once I was released from the hospital, I didn't want them to tamper with my scars. Does that make sense? I felt like I owed her these scars."

He was silent for a long moment, and she thought he wasn't going to answer her question about the older girl, thought that maybe the lack of a reply was his answer, when he finished dully, "Hobbs got around me somehow. He got the older girl out. She was badly burned, but she survived."

She held on to him. What else could she do? She had no words to make him understand that it wasn't his fault, that even being the best sometimes wasn't enough. So she held on.

Someone behind them coughed. Seth lifted his head.

One second his arms clung to her. The next, they hurled her away, throwing her to the ground. Sophie heard two more soft, quick coughs as she landed, painfully hard, on her elbow and her hip. The pain sent shooting stars up to her shoulder and down to her wrist and she stared up at Seth as he staggered back, his face going slack and startled, and she didn't understand. Even when a tremendous noise—*a gunshot?*—echoed through the hollow atrium and Seth jerked, then sank, slowly and uncertainly, to his knees, she didn't understand what was happening, what had happened.

And when she saw Tom standing to the left and behind Seth, his gun still raised, his mouth snarling something she didn't take in, she still didn't understand, except that Seth lay on his back now and she was moving, scrambling over next to him, disregarding the pain of new injuries and old ones.

His eyes were closed. The circle of blood on the shoulder of his blue shirt was the size of a silver dollar. Her frantic hands touched him—his chest, his arms, the pulse in his throat.

He opened his eyes. "Dammit," he said, his voice weak but clear. "Get down. Did Tom shoot that bastard?"

Tom? The wet, red circle on his shirt was as big as her fist now, and growing. *Tom shot* . . . she had to clench her distraught hands into fists to keep them from trying to scoop up the spreading blood and push it back into him. *Tom shot you,* she almost said, but belatedly her brain processed the sounds she'd been hearing all along, for the past twenty or thirty incredibly long seconds, and she darted one quick look around.

North's man was on the floor, like Seth. Shot? About twenty feet away, next to one of the hallways that radiated off the atrium, Tom held his gun on a small man in a brown suit, telling him again to put down his weapon, that he was under arrest. And the man in the brown suit was bending, laying something on the floor—a gun. A funny-looking gun with something on the barrel. A silencer?

"Yes," she said as, all at once, the events snapped into place. "Tom has him." She understood now. Brown Suit had tried to kill her. Seth had seen something—the assassin shooting North's man, probably—and he'd thrown Sophie down. Tom had arrived at that moment and fired at Brown Suit.

And the man lying on the floor, bleeding and hurt, had saved her. Again. "I didn't fail this time," he said weakly, and smiled.

"Damn you," she said as the tears broke free and she pulled off her soft white vest, folding it to make a bandage for the spreading crimson on his shoulder. "Don't you dare smile at me like that."

Sophie tried not to see the other people in the surgical waiting room. She especially tried not to see Tom, who sat on the other side of the small room with its horridly cheerful yellow walls. Tom hadn't looked at her since they reached the hospital and began waiting.

They heard about North's man first, since he wasn't badly hurt. Apparently he'd been wearing a bulletproof vest, standard policy with that agency for high-risk assignments. The force of the bullet had still hit him like a hammer blow, cracking a rib and causing extensive bruising, but the main reason the man had been out of commission during the brief encounter with the gunman was that he'd just plain had the breath knocked out of him.

Seth was undergoing exploratory surgery. After some endless period of time passed, a friendly woman with red hair and stained teeth tried to talk to Sophie about her son, who was having his appendix removed. Sophie wanted to scream at her.

Instead, she looked at the woman blankly and nodded or smiled a few times, then said "Excuse me" and went to the ladies' room. She thought she might throw up but she didn't, though she stayed in there a long time.

When she opened the ladies' room door, Raz stood directly outside. He grinned unevenly. "Thank God you came out," he said. "I thought I'd have to go in after you."

She stopped dead. "Did you—have you heard anything?" Why else would Raz be waiting for her?

He shook his head and reached for her arm. "I just got here. They had a little trouble finding me." He pulled gently, and she followed him back down the wide, white hall. "Tom said you'd been gone awhile. He was worried, so I came to make sure you were okay."

Tom was worried? Oh, sure. She was responsible for his cousin being in surgery at this moment, and he was worried about her?

"Seth will be fine, Sophie," Raz said gently. "The doctor didn't think there was much damage. He just had to look to be sure."

"Of course he will be," she agreed automatically. "But any surgery is a risk. Do you know how many things can go wrong just with the anesthetic? And the surgeon. I didn't ever meet him. Even Tom didn't get to talk to him because they were in a hurry, and he had to sign the forms. What do we know about the surgeon? Is he any good?"

Raz muttered something that damned his brother for an idiot as they turned the corner. "I know the idea of Seth being shot is scary, but the bullet isn't in a tricky location, and . . ."

She didn't hear the rest of his words. Tom came out of the waiting room, his hat in his hand. He was obviously looking for them, and her feet stopped moving as fear once again welled up in her.

"There you are," he said, and in a few quick strides he'd joined them. "Look, Sophia—Miss Cochran—I know you don't want to be around me," he said, his hands—big hands, she noticed, very much like Seth's—turning his black Stetson around and around. "I can understand that, under the circumstances. If it bothers you so much you have to go hide out in the ladies' room to get away from me, I'll wait somewhere else."

It took a second for her mind to catch up with what he was saying. "What are you talking about?" she asked.

Raz muttered something about "damn fool."

He scowled. "You blame me for Seth getting shot. I can't argue. I should have realized that the killer could have arrived at that office complex ahead of you and been waiting inside the building. I was inexcusably careless."

"You're an idiot," Raz told him. "You know that? All this wallowing around in guilt is useless. You couldn't know they had a wireless tap on her phone. You've had the neighborhood watched, and there weren't any suspicious vans or parked cars for them to monitor her calls from."

The strain on Tom's face didn't lessen, but the focus of his eyes changed, as if he were looking outward again. "Since her phone was definitely monitored, and from nearby, it looks like one of her neighbors was helping Rios, doesn't it?"

Raz nodded. "That will bear looking into. Madison's denying everything, but it won't do him any good. In addition to the drug-trafficking charges the DEA has stuck on him, it looks like we'll get him for contract murder. Rios panicked when he realized the feds were taking his boss down."

"Rios is talking?" Tom asked.

"Singing high and loud. The D.A.'s office moved fast on the deal you suggested. I'd like to know how you rate that kind of—"

"Hold on," Sophie said, waving her hands as she tried to sort through what she'd been hearing. "Hold on, will you? Who's Rios? And Madison—he's been arrested?"

Both men looked at her. "Rios is the man who tried to kill you," Tom said bluntly. "He's turned state's evidence against Madison, which gives us one more charge to stick the bastard with. The feds were planning to move against Madison today anyway. After sifting through the results of several months of investigation, they had decided they had enough to put the man out of business."

"Tom isn't good with explanations," Raz interjected, exasperated. "Madison is under arrest because Tom lit a fire under a few people who'd been dragging their tails in the DEA."

"Don't be a jackass," Tom said impatiently. "Special Investigations has been the liaison in this investigation. In that respect it occurred to me that the various people involved in the case hadn't gotten together to discuss it for some time, that's all. After some discussion everyone decided there was solid, well-documented evidence on the drug-related charges, and getting him on Farquhar's murder wasn't necessary. The upshot for you, Sophie, is that Madison will be too busy to worry about you, especially since he isn't being charged with Farquhar's murder. Between Rios, the federal courts, and the business rival of Madison's who supplied us with much of our evidence, the man has plenty of problems," Tom finished with satisfaction.

So she was safe. Sophie tested the idea in her mind, but her thoughts couldn't settle, jittering from one idea to the next, then back to the center of her worries. She licked her lips. "I thought you were avoiding me because it's my fault," she told Tom. "What happened to Seth is my fault, not yours." And Seth deserved better, so much better, than her.

His face got a sharp, arrested look. She thought he was about to speak when the door to the waiting room opened.

The thin, dark man who stepped out into the hall wore the green scrubs of a surgeon. Sophie's heart stopped.

"Lieutenant Rasmussin?" the tired-looking man in the green scrubs said, glancing between Raz and Tom. "Is one of you Seth Brogan's cousin?"

"We're both his cousins," Tom said, "but I'm the lieutenant."

"Good enough. I'm Dr. Diaz. Mr. Brogan's surgery went smoothly. We took a little longer than we'd originally thought because the bullet passed so close to the bone. I wanted to be sure it hadn't nicked a little chip or two off. But Mr. Brogan is extremely lucky. The bullet passed through his shoulder cleanly. We'll want to keep him overnight to be sure there's no infection. He's in recovery now. You can go see him there in about fifteen minutes, if you wish."

The doctor's voice faded to a distant buzzing in her ears as Sophie's fear drained away in a rush. She swayed on her feet. Someone's arm came around her waist, supporting her, and she blinked a few times. Gradually her senses stabilized, so that she heard the doctor and Tom settling it that she would be the one allowed to go see Seth in recovery.

And the fear flooded back in. "No." Frantically she shoved at the arm supporting her—Raz's arm, she realized—and reeled back. "Oh, no. I can't. It wouldn't be right. You go, Tom. Or Raz. One of you go see him." And she spun away from their astonished faces, hurrying off on unsteady legs before they could stop her.

The windows in the hospital cafeteria were dark, Sophie noted with vague surprise. It must be night. She wondered how long she'd been sitting there. The cold cup of coffee in front of her gave no clue. She thought it had probably been there awhile.

A loaded cafeteria tray landed on the table next to her. She jumped.

"Sorry to startle you," Tom's voice said from behind her. He moved into view from her left. "You've got your choice.

One of those sandwiches is supposed to be ham. The other's corned beef.'' He pulled out the chair next to her and sat down. Something about him looked different, but she wasn't sure what it was. "They probably both taste like cardboard smeared with mustard, but eat one anyway.''

Businesslike, his hands began sorting through the contents of his tray. He set one of the sandwiches in front of her, along with some chips and a carton of milk. "I think you've got the ham,'' he said. "If you'd rather have corned beef, speak up now.'' He began unwrapping his sandwich.

She shook her head in bewilderment. Something was definitely different about him. "Why are you doing this? After I... after the way I treated Seth.'' *It's better this way,* she reminded herself. Seth wouldn't want her anymore after the way she'd run out on him. He would start getting over her.

He looked at her out of pale, expressionless eyes. "Why haven't you left the hospital?''

She just shook her head.

"Eat,'' he told her. "We'll talk after you've gotten some food in you.''

"I already ate.''

"No, you didn't. Raz and I have been checking on you ever since you took off down that hall. You've been down here, and you haven't done anything but buy coffee you throw away without drinking, and use the phone. Calling to see about Seth, I figure.'' Maybe she imagined the softening in his expression. "He's doing fine, Sophie. He's asleep in his room now, or he was when I left. Raz is with him.''

She was so drained, so confused. Why would Raz and Tom have kept checking on her? When he again ordered her to eat she obeyed, mostly because it seemed easier.

To her surprise, she was able to eat about half the sandwich without much effort. Maybe she had been hungry, or at least in need of fuel. She didn't think she could eat the other half, though. She wrapped it back up, glancing at Tom.

He'd finished his sandwich and most of the chips while she was eating. "I was right," he said, shaking his milk carton to see if any was left. She thought it an incongruous sight—milk went with cookies and little boys, not with grizzled timber wolves. "It did taste like cardboard. Feel a little better now?"

She nodded, glancing at the dark mirror that night made of the windows. She wished Tom would go away.

"You've been stuck down here long enough," he said, standing. "Let's walk."

"But I—" His hand at her elbow urged her to stand. She winced. It was her left elbow, the one she'd landed on. She stood quickly, pulling away. She'd go with him, and let him get this talk over with. It seemed the best way to get rid of him.

"Sorry," he said. "Your arm is sore? Both arms, now? You and Seth will make quite a pair," he said as he took her arm and steered her toward glass doors that opened onto a small courtyard that held a few metal tables and chairs. It was dimly lit by the glass-walled expanse of the cafeteria. "Both of you banged up and hobbling around. You're limping!" He observed her carefully as she came outside. "I hadn't realized you hurt your leg. Maybe you should get it looked at."

"It's my hip, and it's bruised, that's all," she said, speaking as stiffly as she was moving. The little courtyard was dark, wet and deserted, but at least the rain had stopped. "Look, I don't understand why you're doing this. Why are you being nice to me?"

He tipped his head back, and that's when she realized what was different. He didn't have his hat. "Aside from what Seth would want, I owe you this, and more. If I hadn't been so involved with my own guilt over letting Seth take that bullet, I would have seen how busily you were blaming yourself. I know why I feel responsible. It's my job to figure the angles, and I missed one. Why do you think it was your fault?"

He sounded serious, as if he really wanted to know. She looked away. Water dripped somewhere nearby. Her hip throbbed. So did her arm, the one she hadn't wanted to wear a sling for this morning. God, what a long time ago that seemed. She raised a shaky hand to cradle her aching arm against her and spoke. "Isn't it obvious? I should never have let him come to Houston with me. You knew that. You pointed it out."

"That isn't what I said. I said you hadn't tried very hard to stop him from coming. I didn't know, at the time, if that was because you needed someone on your side and didn't mind using Seth, or because you genuinely cared about him."

"Now you know," she said bitterly, stepping farther into the shadows. "Go away, Tom. If you felt some duty to see that I didn't faint from hunger, you've taken care of it. Now go away."

"He asked about you when he woke up. First in recovery, then up in his room. He doesn't understand why you haven't been to see him."

She stopped moving. Her eyes closed tight on her pain.

"He saved your life." Tom's voice told her that he'd followed her. "And you feel guilty. You think everything that happened was your fault. I admit that for a while I thought that was why you couldn't go see him, because all you had to offer him was guilt. But that wasn't the feeling I saw on your face when you ran away, Sophie. What I saw on your face was fear, pure and simple. And I guess it wouldn't be surprising if, after losing your parents, then your sister, you were afraid to care deeply again."

He paused for a long moment. Probably he wanted her to respond. She did manage to turn around, to look at him, and her mouth opened, but she couldn't speak, couldn't manage to string two thoughts together in the wake of the vast astonishment she felt.

When he spoke again, his voice was rough with some emotion she couldn't read on his craggy face. "I'm going up to Seth's room now, so Raz can come down and eat one of those cardboard and mustard sandwiches. I'll tell Raz to give you a ride home.'' He hesitated. ''Goodbye, Sophie.''

She heard his boots rapping against the concrete, and she heard the door open, then close, but even though she was facing that way, she didn't see Tom leave. She was too filled with what he'd said. *Fear, pure and simple.* The words reverberated inside her, growing larger and larger.

Fear? Was that, could that, be true, be the real reason she was willing to hurt Seth—was it as simple, as ignoble, as fear? Had she hung on to the guilt because it was easier to face than the truth? Not because she didn't deserve him, wasn't worthy of his love, nothing so exalted or unselfish, but purely because she was... terrified.

It was a good thing the little courtyard was deserted, and that the lights from the cafeteria reached outside only dimly. Because after a while she began to laugh, and to cry, both mixed up together in a way that would have looked demented if anyone had been watching.

Seth was glad he had a private room. If he had to be in a hospital again, at least he could turn off the noise of the television and stare out the window, undisturbed by a roommate who was too sick, too talkative, or who otherwise intruded on Seth's unquiet mind.

Not that he could escape every invasion. Nurses came and went with their needles and pills and less dignified instruments. Even the sunshine that had opened this day, that beamed gently in on him now, was an intrusion if you didn't want it. And Seth didn't. He closed his eyes against the damned sunshine.

He'd wanted Sophie with him after he came around from the surgery yesterday, but he'd been too drugged to fret about her absence for long. For a while last night the knowledge that she was safe, that this time he hadn't failed, had sustained him. But he was a selfish man. Just knowing she was alive hadn't been enough for long. He wanted her here, with him.

He was extremely lucky. He knew that, even if he couldn't summon the proper gratitude. Absolutely nothing major had been damaged by the bullet, and they were kicking him out this afternoon with a supply of antibiotics and instructions to come back in seventy-two hours to get the wound checked.

He didn't bother to open his eyes when he heard the door open, then close. "They still haven't found the admission form you signed," he told Tom. "That little aide left to get me another one to fill out. I guess I could use some help getting my pants on while we wait, if you don't mind."

"I don't mind," said a voice that absolutely did not belong to Tom, "if you don't."

He opened his eyes. And saw her. Just as he'd longed to see her last night, and hadn't. Like he'd prayed to see her this morning. And hadn't. He didn't answer. Just watched her hesitant advance.

"I've arranged for a proper hospital bed to be set up in one of the guest rooms," she said. "And a nurse. You have to have a nurse, Seth. Tom's been helping me by dragging things out here so I'd have time to get ready for you to—to come home with me."

Hope, he discovered, had the kick of a mule. It knocked the breath right out of him. He managed one word. "Bossy."

Hope, on her face, looked like the sun coming out. "I'm not taking over," she assured him, "any more than you were when you arranged for those security people at my house. Seth . . ." She reached one hand out to him as she stopped next to his bed, then let it fall. "I'm sorry. So sorry. I was a fool to think of leaving you." She frowned, her half-moon eyebrows lowering to crescents. "Don't tell me it's too late, Seth Brogan. Just because I've been an idiot doesn't mean you should be one, too. Besides, you didn't make things easy on me, you know. Do you have any idea how hard it is on us ordinary mortals, being around a hero?''

"Sophie," he said, finding his breath and his smile at the same time, "sit down. You're babbling."

She did sit. But instead of pulling a chair close, she eased herself up onto the bed with him, as finicky and careful in her movements as a cat settling into some new place. The sunlight that before had been so unwelcome now gladdened him by burnishing her hair to gold.

She laid her fingers, light as a kiss, on the uninjured side of his chest. "I know you don't see yourself as a hero, but believe me, it's perfectly obvious to everyone else. Good grief, you took the bullet meant for me."

His newborn hope faltered. "If you've come because you're grateful—"

"Oh, no. I probably ought to be grateful, but the fact is, once I got over the shock of realizing why I've been trying so hard to close you out, I was really mad at you for getting yourself shot like that. No, Seth, I realize that if I love you I'm going to have to accept your difficult qualities along with your good ones, but—"

But he didn't let her say any more. One of his arms, at least, was working, and she was right there next to him, so it was wonderfully easy to pull her to him and kiss the pretty mouth that had at last, at long last, said the words he needed. Then, when he had completely stolen her breath and her reason with the fine, mute persuasions of his tongue, when she hung noodle-limp in his good arm, he demanded, "Say it again. Without the 'if' in front of it."

She blinked dazed green eyes at him. "I love you."

So he kissed her again.

Sophie hardly noticed as they sank onto his bed together. The feelings overwhelming her were so much stronger than fear—luscious, life-celebrating feelings. She gave him, and his kiss, everything she had.

They ended up more or less horizontal in his bed, breathing heavily. Sophie curled up against his "good" side, well away from his wound, which meant, ironically, that she was on his left side. The one with the scars. "So," he said, his breath still huffing in and out audibly, sounding achingly happy. "You are going to marry me, aren't you?"

She smiled. "Thank goodness you proposed. I was afraid I'd have to do it myself, and coming here today and telling you I wasn't going to let you go has used up my courage for the next week or two."

"You've got courage enough for anyone," he told her huskily, toying with a strand of her hair. "Maybe you'll start believing me about that one of these days."

Sophie didn't argue. She didn't even try to explain how terrifying it was for her to love a man like him: a real hero, a man who naturally went around saving her, and saving others, too. Getting himself badly, permanently, hurt because he was the sort of man who would always help someone in trouble, whether they were strangers in a burning building, an ugly, pregnant dog, or a woman so lost she didn't even know her name.

"I'd rather not sell my cabin," he said, toying with her hair. "Maybe we can go there for weekends sometimes?"

"Wait a minute." She managed to get herself partly upright, though it wasn't easy with one elbow sore and the upper arm on her other side still tender. "You sound like you're planning to live here. In Houston."

He smiled. "Did you think I'd insist you give up your home? I'm not so selfish. I know your home is important, something that has been in your family for years—"

"And I've been negotiating for two months to turn it into a second home for the children's group I work with, but it looks like my neighbors have me blocked on zoning. That house isn't home to me anymore, Seth. It hasn't been for some time. I'll probably sell it and use the proceeds to finance the children's home I have in mind." She smiled. "Did you think I was so selfish I'd take you away from the home you built with your own two hands? Seth, I love your cabin."

He stared at her a moment, then began to laugh.

The sound startled her. She realized she'd never heard him laugh before. The sound of his laughter was full bellied, entrancing. She giggled, then laughed out loud. "We're both so damned noble," she managed to say.

"Aren't we, though?" He relaxed back against his pillow with a sigh. "It doesn't matter where we live, does it? I think, maybe, I need to come down from my mountain for a while. I think..." He hesitated, then continued, "I may want to settle in that area eventually, keep up with my naturalism, but if I stay here for a couple years I can finish the degree I'll need to become a fire marshal, or maybe to train fire fighters back in the Fort Davis area."

She hugged him, so happy for him, for this sign that his ghosts were finally resting easier, that she couldn't speak at first. She hoped they would spend a lot of time at the cabin, but if he needed to be away from it for a while, that was good, too. She knew she'd have the piercing clarity of starshine whenever she needed it by looking into Seth's eyes, and the clean air of the heights whenever she breathed in his scent while he held her, like this, in his arms. Because Seth carried his mountain with him, inside.

She was beginning to understand that she had her own mountain, too, a place of heights and courage still mostly unexplored. "It doesn't matter," she agreed. "We'll work the details out."

He held her a few minutes then in silence, the two of them enraptured with being together, with being alive in spite of everything. "Sophie," he said as he'd said once before— only once, "I love you."

And she smiled.

* * * * *

SILHOUETTE® Desire®

COMING NEXT MONTH

#1009 THE COWBOY AND THE KID—Anne McAllister
July's *Man of the Month*, rodeo cowboy Taggart Jones, vowed never to remarry, but his little girl had other plans for him—and every one involved feisty schoolmarm Felicity Albright.

#1010 A GIFT FOR BABY—Raye Morgan
The Baby Shower
All Hailey Kingston wanted was to go to her friend's baby shower. Instead, she was stuck on a remote ranch, with a handsome cowboy as her keeper. But the longer she stayed in Mitch Harper's arms, the less she wanted to leave!

#1011 THE BABY NOTION—Dixie Browning
Daddy Knows Last
Priscilla Barrington wanted a baby, so she planned a visit to the town sperm bank. But then she met Jake Spencer! Could she convince the rugged cowboy to father her child—the old-fashioned way?

#1012 THE BRIDE WORE BLUE—Cindy Gerard
Northern Lights Brides
When Maggie Adams returned home, she never expected to see her childhood neighbor Blue Hazzard. Could the former gawky teenager turned hunk teach Maggie how to love again?

#1013 GAVIN'S CHILD—Caroline Cross
Bachelors and Babies
Gavin Cantrell was stunned to return home and learn that his estranged wife Annie had given birth to his child without telling him. Now that he was back, would his dream of being a family man be fulfilled?

#1014 MONTANA FEVER—Jackie Merritt
Made in Montana
Independent Lola Fanon never met anyone as infuriating—or as irresistible—as Duke Sheridan. She knew he wasn't her type, but staying away from the handsome rancher was becoming a losing battle....

Take 4 bestselling love stories FREE

Plus get a FREE surprise gift!

SILHOUETTE DESIRE® "CELEBRATION 1000" SWEEPSTAKES
OFFICIAL RULES—NO PURCHASE NECESSARY

To enter, complete an Official Entry Form or a 3"x5" card by hand printing "Silhouette Desire Celebration 1000 Sweepstakes," your name and address, and mail it to: In the U.S.: Silhouette Desire Celebration 1000 Sweepstakes, P.O. Box 9069, Buffalo, NY 14269-9069, or in Canada: Silhouette Desire Celebration 1000 Sweepstakes, P.O. Box 637, Fort Erie, Ontario L2A 5X3. Limit one entry per envelope. Entries must be sent via first-class mail and be received no later than 6/30/96. No liability is assumed for lost, late or misdirected mail.

Prizes: Grand Prize—an original painting (approximate value $1500 U.S.);300 Runner-up Prizes—an autographed Silhouette Desire® Book (approximate value $3.50 U.S./$3.99 CAN. each). Winners will be selected in a random drawing (to be conducted no later than 9/30/96) from among all eligible entries received by D.L. Blair, Inc., an independent judging organization whose decision is final.

Sweepstakes offer is open only to residents of the U.S. (except Puerto Rico) and Canada who are 18 years of age or older, except employees and immediate family members of Harlequin Enterprises Ltd., their affiliates, subsidiaries, and all agencies, entities and persons connected with the use, marketing or conduct of this sweepstakes. All federal, state, provincial, municipal and local laws apply. Offer void where prohibited by law. Taxes and/or duties are the sole responsibility of the winners. Any litigation within the province of Quebec respecting the conduct and awarding of prizes may be submitted to the Regie des alcools des courses et des jeux. All prizes will be awarded; winners will be notified by mail. No substitution for prizes is permitted. Odds of winning are dependent upon the number of eligible entries received.

Grand Prize winner must sign and return an Affidavit of Eligibility within 30 days of notification. In the event of noncompliance within this time period, prize may be awarded to an alternate winner. Any prize or prize notification returned as undeliverable may result in the awarding of that prize to an alternate winner. By acceptance of their prize, winners consent to the use of their names, photographs or likenesses for purposes of advertising, trade and promotion on behalf of Harlequin Enterprises Ltd., without further compensation unless prohibited by law. In order to win a prize, residents of Canada will be required to correctly answer a time-limited arithmetical skill-testing question administered by mail.

For a list of winners (available after October 31, 1996) send a separate self-addressed stamped envelope to: Silhouette Desire Celebration 1000 Sweepstakes Winners, P.O. Box 4200, Blair, NE 68009-4200.

SWEEPR

SILHOUETTE®

Desire®

CELEBRATION 1000

A treasured piece of romance could be yours!

During April, May and June as part of
Desire's Celebration 1000 you can enter to win an
original piece of art used on an actual Desire cover!

Or you could win one of 300 autographed Man of the
Month books!

See Official Sweepstakes Rules for more details.

To enter, complete an Official Entry Form or a 3"x5" card by hand printing
"Silhouette Desire Celebration 1000 Sweepstakes", your name and address, and
mail to: **In the U.S.:** Silhouette Desire Celebration 1000 Sweepstakes, P.O. Box
9069, Buffalo, N.Y. 14269-9069, or **In Canada:** Silhouette Desire Celebration 1000
Sweepstakes, P.O. Box 637, Fort Erie, Ontario L2A 5X3. Limit one entry per
envelope. Entries must be sent via first-class mail and be received no later than
6/30/96. No liability is assumed for lost, late or misdirected mail.

**Official Entry Form—Silhouette Desire Celebration 1000
Sweepstakes**

Name: _____

Address: _____

City: _____

State/Province: _____

Zip or Postal Code: _____

Favorite Desire Author: _____

Favorite Desire Book: _____

SWEEPS

Silhouette's recipe for a sizzling summer:

* Take the best-looking cowboy in South Dakota
* Mix in a brilliant bachelor
* Add a sexy, mysterious sheikh
* Combine their stories into one collection and you've got one sensational super-hot read!

Summer Sizzlers

MEN OF Summer

Three short stories by these favorite authors:

Kathleen Eagle
Joan Hohl
Barbara Faith

Available this July wherever
Silhouette books are sold.

Look us up on-line at: http://www.romance.net

Silhouette®

SS96